M.R. ERFMAN

Lilith

Mr. M's Bookshop Vol. 1

First edition

ISBN: 979-8-9912621-0-1

This book was professionally typeset on Reedsy.
Find out more at reedsy.com

To My Great Grandmother Lily,
Thank you for teaching me
that in the face of adversity,
all we have is to be strong.
I wish you and Aunt Gloria were here to see this...

Warning

Vol. 1 Lilith is a dark paranormal romance novel and is intended for **mature audiences only**. For those who would like to review the content before reading, please see the complete list in the back of the book.

For those who are reading this and think "fuck that surprise me!"

Same...

"Into a place I came
Where light was silent all.
Bellowing there groan'd
A noise, as of a sea in tempest torn
By warring winds.
The stormy blast of hell
With restless fury drives the spirits on,
Whirl'd round and dash'd amain with sore annoy.
When the arrive before the ruinous sweep,
There shrieks are heard, their laminations, moans,
And blasphemies 'gainst the Good Power of heaven.
The carnal sinners are condemn'd, in whom
Reason Lust is sway'd…"
Dante Alighieri's Inferno Canto V

In the Beginning

Many learned the difference between good and evil as a child. Convinced by the Bible that, in the beginning, it took six days for God to create all we know, which was good. He worked tirelessly on making the land and sea, animals and plants, light and darkness. All this pulled from within the Void.

However, the Void was never able to tell Her story. What they don't write in the books is that She is omniscient as well. She is a never-ending entity that holds all the universe's light within herself.

God pulled so much from the Void that She became restive. With each creation, God didn't grab from nothing. He stole from her delicate, irreplaceable purity. The Void was just as masterful, if not more than God. Without the Void's stolen sacrifices, God would have created nothing.

Patiently, the Void waited as She watched God work. For six days, She methodically planned her prospective creations. She observed every tiny detail to produce something far grander in her design. The more God robbed her soul, the more She felt things differently than when she was whole. He cared not for how he used her. His only regard was that she was there as an instrument to use.

The first beast The Void created, She pulled her desires together. Every primal craving She could imagine. Love, hunger, yearning, wishes, delights, and interests were placed collectively and formed a magnificent allure.

She designed this beast to compel God's image of himself to seek it out endlessly, just as He continuously sought out from her. The beast could take the shape of his desires and steal away their vitality as they slept.

Shadows of the Void's edges came together to make its vessel. The Void looked upon Her creation, and She was happy. She knew she created pure darkness and cast it down to the earth.

Busy as He was, God did not see the beast watching and anxiously awaiting its ultimate form. On the sixth day, with divine intent, he reached his hand into the damp soil and sculpted a being in his image. As he finished with the final touches, He placed the being gently on the Earth and called it man.

The Earth called to God once more. Unable to resist, He bore his fingers again into the ground and, at God's hand, unknowingly started forming the Void's beast. It became the most beautiful creature of Her image. With long flowing hair and eyes that masqueraded innocence, God placed the beast gently on the earth and called it woman.

God rested on the seventh day, and the Void smiled as She watched her vengeance unfold.

1

Lily

Hunger is an illustrious equalizer. No matter the creature, we all experience the emptiness it has to offer. Sometimes, the relentless petition from my hollow belly is easily satisfied. Like yesterday, I devoured a bag of Dino nuggets, granted I felt like shit afterward. However, other times, it feels like my particular cravings will consume me completely, and if I don't eat soon, I'm not sure who I will hurt.

No matter what I eat or how much, it never really satisfies me. I could go to a Chinese buffet, eat ten plates, and still be hungry. It is one of the many things that Adam fell in love with me for. Something about a girl not fearing her waist size and devouring everything she wanted turned him on at first.

My older sister once said that I have a unique sense of smell. I could pick out the horniest man at the club whenever we went. It's the perfect skill when all you're trying to do is get laid and go home. Although, it tends to get weird on occasion.

This one time, I decided to try out the mechanical bull at this cowboy club. There was an old guy; all wrinkles, no teeth.

Granted, he would have been an easy meal, but I just can't. For fucks sake, my head will explode if I don't get something to eat soon.

"Hey babe, do you know what you want to do for our anniversary?" a sultry voice says from behind me. Right on cue. I'm starting to get cold standing here naked after my shower, and a girl can only take so long to get ready. Despite Adam's thin figure, he is like a furnace. Adam slips his arms around my naked waist and bends down to rest his chin on my shoulder, his tawny beige skin contrasts my pale complexion. His jade green eyes pull me in, melting away memories of our past. For now, I feel like I can forgive each one of Adam's sins.

It's nice sometimes to have a man that is taller than you. Comparing myself to most women I am far from short. Adam's wavy brown hair falls to the side, tickling my arm. I giggle as the full deep brown beard on his face brushes against my neck as Adam kisses it playfully.

"Honestly, babe, I have to think about it later." I layer a pouty tone in my voice. His lust is so palatable right now. It's too distracting for me to think about a date night. I'm starving, and he smells like chocolate cake. I love chocolate cake, both literally and not quite literally. My waist size shows that I enjoy eating as much as I do physical activity.

"That's fine. I'm going to make some breakfast here in a minute. Do you want some eggs?" The vibration of his voice hitting my skin almost tickles. I press my ass into his groin. No matter what comes out of this man's mouth, he has my full attention.

"I think I could go for a side of you right now," I coo. My cold, calculating brown eyes reflect back at me from the mirror, their dark depths nearly devoid of emotion as I stare hungrily at Adam.

Primal hunger incites me. I push my ass into his groin again, adding more pressure as I twist around. Lingering on the delicate curve of his perfect lips. My desperate glare traces the lines of his toned muscular body with an intensity that borders on obsession. Following every slope and hill of his chiseled build, my breath quickens with the rising pulse hammering in my chest. I flash a well practiced soft smile and gingerly push him backward onto the chair we keep in the bathroom for moments like this.

"Well, this isn't what I had in mind," Adam grabs hold of my chin, "but if you insist," he growls. I reach down and unzip his pants, making a show of it. With raw desire, I push Adam's pants and boxers smoothly over his heavenly ass. His erection pops out, ready to dive into the possibilities that lie ahead. I kiss him gingerly in a straight line down his bare chest and washboard abs, taking a moment to appreciate the meal before me.

It's satisfying to know that after everything we've been through, his cock still gets hard for me. As I run my nails down the sides of his body, Adam arches slightly into them, deepening my graze. The smell of chocolate cake intensifies as he shivers under my hands.

Thank you, Lord, for this meal I'm about to eat; because I'm fucking starving. Adam holds his cock upright, lining it with my mouth. Drool pools under my tongue as I slide it to the back of my throat. Carefully, I wrap my lips around the base, letting my saliva moisten every inch to glide it in and out flawlessly. His cock becomes more demanding in my mouth. I gag at its girth, forcing it down my throat.

Adam's moans fill the open space around us, driving my

need for satisfaction higher. I reach between my legs and rub my fingers across my clit. I'm so wet and needy that I'm dripping. I can't wait. I hunger.

With a pop, I let go of my mouth's stronghold on him and crawl onto his lap. If I wasn't so ravenous, I would be more concerned about breaking Adam from being on top. His hands grip my hips as he licks his lips and guides himself into me inch by blessed inch, drawing it out as slowly as possible so I can feel how much he fills me. He knows too well that this is my favorite part.

The sated sensation of him coaxes a fervid cry from my mouth. I dig my nails into his shoulders, savoring our growing friction. Adam takes hold of my hips fiercely and sets me at a breathtaking pace. His complete control of the tempo amplifies my need with every stroke.

I can feel his cock pulsing inside me, tickling parts I dream I could reach alone. Hastily, pulling me up and down. Adam leans back into a bridge, suspending me off the chair. Holding me there for a moment, Adam pulls back. He slams into me viciously, driving my arousal through the roof. Electricity shoots throughout my body.

Our quickie changes me from pleasure to predator. Biting his neck hard causes Adam to toss his head back, "Fuck Lily!" He screams, pulling out of me, grabbing my torso to the point of subtle pain, and flips me around onto my hands and knees like a rag-doll. I find my footing and open my legs. "You want to be rough? I'll fucking show you rough." Adam smacks my ass cheek, shooting a burning pain through it. With one hand, he latches onto my shoulder, squeezing tight, and the other stays on my hip. Adam drives into me with forceful, rhythmic motion.

Ensuring I get precisely what is needed, I pant, "There, right there, don't stop!" I plant my face into the chair, wrapping my hands behind my back. Adam takes hold, raggedly burying himself harder and harder into me. With a final thrust, Adam pushes himself deep inside as he spills over. As he lets go, I get up and push him back onto the chair. The legs of it screech off of the white tile floor.

This is going to be a decent feeding. I need this. Give me this. I take control, sheathing him once more, and drive my hips onto Adam's lap while simultaneously grinding my clit on him. Adam barely grows firmer within me. Moving my hands from the back of the chair to Adam's face, I run my tongue over his, moaning at the taste of fresh strawberries.

Coaxing my meal from his lips, chasing my orgasm, I fiercely inhale the beautiful mist of various shades of blue, finally silencing my hunger pangs.

Consuming his lust throws me over the edge of my pleasure. I clamp down on what's left of his erection until I get every last drop.

The feast breathes new life into me. I rise with the intention of showering again but Adam snags my wrist before I can dismount. He pulls me back down to him, more ambitious than I'm used to expecting. "You ruin me, woman." Adam's sharp eyes command my attention. Resting my forehead on his, intensifying his despotic eyes by blocking out the light.

I lean in close to his ear whispering, "Without you, I would starve." I lick my lips, wishing for more. Anything more he can offer up as I twist my wrist out of his grasp.

It's enough to survive. However, living life, consuming only minuscule repast has its own set of consequences. As I pick myself back up and walk to the porcelain sink, my stomach gurgles confirming that I'm also hungry for actual food. "Can you make us breakfast? I'm dying for some pancakes." I usually make breakfast for us, but today I need to get more out of him other than food. One round just isn't enough. Besides, regardless of his answer, I'll have to take another shower and clean up our mess. It would be nice to get a break from that routine.

"Unless…" I pause hoping he will take the bait. His eyes darken and scan my body, sending chills through it. I pray he can go another round. I could use a second course. The overwhelming hunger may have subsided, but the deep wanting for more has me feeling hollow.

Adam grabs the towel that hangs on the back of the bathroom door. Watching him wipe any evidence of me off himself, tugging on his partially swollen cock has me chewing on my bottom lip. Disappointment stabs at me as he tosses it to the side. Without a word, Adam pulls up and buttons his pants.

He leaves the bathroom, and I hear his footsteps stomping down the stairs. I yell out the door, "Can't blame a girl for trying!" The exhaustion that weighed me down this morning feels slightly lifted. It could be worse. At least I got some this morning instead of waiting until later. Internet yoga has nothing on how my joints feel.

The shower has always been the one place I can go to think. Something about the water helps clear my head better than anything else. My aunt told me that water is cleansing beyond the skin. Life would be so much easier if the jet setting on the shower head would clean me the way I really need it to. I'm still working on that running theory. If I can figure out how to feed off my desire, that would fix all my problems.

Reaching this level of ravenous is new to me. It's as if the older I get, the more I require. Besides, Adam doesn't look like he will last much longer. If this keeps up, I'm not sure what will happen. What if I kill him? Can I kill Adam by feeding from him? What if I'm the reason he has changed so much?

As much as I love him, I won't deny the changes that have been happening. It is as if every time I feed, he loses a little more of himself. That's never happened before with anyone else I have been with.

Thankfully, cleaning myself up in the shower only takes a few seconds, so I have time to be picky with choosing my armor for the day.

You can say that my aunt was always more motherly to me than my own mother. She taught me everything I know when it comes to being a woman. She talked to me about the most important things a young woman should learn, like sex and periods. However, she also gave me some lifelong advice I will never forget. Every day, she would say, *"Lily, you're a beautiful girl who will grow up to be a beautiful woman. Just as a knight has his armor carefully crafted, a woman selects her attire."*

I didn't understand it as a kid. It must be one of those things you grasp onto more firmly as you get older and have lived a little. If my mother had been around, I would have asked her to explain it to me. My mother was so beautiful. She had full, vibrant hair and eyes that commanded the attention of every man. I would always watch her. I wanted to learn how to be pretty like her, though we were nothing alike, so it was kind of a moot point.

When she put on makeup, it was a work of art. She would keep her face expressionless. Stone cold and determined. My mother reminded me of a warrior putting on battle paint. I sometimes catch a glimpse of her in the mirror, within my own features. Though, now all I can see are empty brown eyes that are just a little too big with heavy bags under them, a nose that is too small, lips that could be more full, the threat of a second chin making itself known when I tilt my head down slightly, and dull chestnut color hair that refuses to be tamed. One time, I asked my mother why she makes a face like she is dead, and she gave me this long spiel about how if you pull the skin, you'll get wrinkles.

I can hear her still telling me, *"Never go out without your weapon. As women, our strongest asset is our sex appeal. Without it, we starve. Trust me, baby, I've been there, and what happens next is not pleasant."* That's the last piece of advice I got from her.

That day, she went missing. She didn't come home. My sister and I stayed with my aunt for a while. We did all the right things. We called the police, filed reports, and even put up missing posters. We searched for years and not a single clue.

Over time, my aunt grew cold and distant. What once was a great relationship, morphed into a battle ground. As my sister and I got older my aunt would disappear for days at a time. It was just the two of us. Randomly, my aunt came home after being M.I.A for a week and announced that my sister and I no longer needed to search for our mother. She was found dead on the other side of town frozen to a tree with a bottle in her hand. My sister couldn't handle staying with us after that. Her wanderlust was insatiable and this was the perfect excuse to go. Since mom was dead and I was an adult, there was nothing left to keep her around. A year later, my aunt was found in an alleyway downtown. Overdose.

Surprisingly, my sister showed up at the funeral, which was

fantastic. I was so excited to see her again. We spent the rest of the day after the funeral catching up and swapping stories. It was a marvelous time, despite the reason for her coming to town. Until I learned that everyone I loved was dead or dying. Fuck Cancer. Now, here I am, a proper orphan. Fatherless, motherless, family-less, just scraping by in the love department one day at a time and little of it to spare for myself.

2

Lily

Despite my wonderful meal, I can't help but think about how I'm hurting Adam. It's been three years of feeding from him and only him. This may be the longest monogamous relationship that I have ever been in. Before him, I was polyamorous. It made sense since multiple "meals" a day is a hell of a lot better than only one.

That's how we met. I went to a swingers club with a few partners; not all participated in the playtime, but they were happy to come with me. Plus, the space is fabulous. They have this standing policy where you could bring your booze from home, and their bartenders would serve you. It is so much cheaper than going to a regular club. I would bring all my fixings for Shirley Temples since I don't drink and am particular on the brand of lemon lime soda that I like in it.

Adam was there as a bull, a single guy who wants to join in. The deep richness of his lust felt exhilarating. I couldn't let him go. We met up for a few dates after that night. It took him a little bit to understand my lifestyle choices. Eventually, he joined the polycule.

Over time, he realized that being poly isn't exactly his cup of tea and asked me to be with only him. I was reluctant at first, but I craved his lust more than anyone else.

His lust is like a drug to me. Chocolate cake and strawberries are an irresistible combination with typical food regardless, but tasting it on him takes that flavor to a divine level. So, I agreed.

My partners were upset to see me go. My girlfriend even said he was too emotionally immature to understand how we all worked. Still, in the end, they respected my choice. I guess the addiction gene doesn't fall far from the tree. I'm a junkie for his stuff, and he is most seductively my drug of choice.

As I descend the staircase, each step creaks beneath my feet. I latch onto the railing to guide me down. Clumsy and stairs don't mix really well. The smell of coffee from the kitchen greets me as I reach the bottom.

I'm not a huge coffee fan, but I drink it at home since Adam doesn't like the smell of tea. He refuses to even let me keep it in the house. I would much rather have a cup of tea in the morning than that.

I spot Adam setting the table as I walk into the kitchen. The toll of our relationship painted all over his face kills me. He's aged twice as fast as anyone I've ever met. There's even a difference this morning.

His grip gets rougher the longer we are together. I know that I'm the one hurting him. Everything he does is because of me and what I am.

I wish I could find something other than him to satiate my appetite so this could work. I hate how I've changed him so much. Adam places an omelet in front of me. For someone who survives on sex, I shouldn't be picky, but I really hate eggs.

They are the most revolting thing on this planet, smelling of pure sulfur.

I catch a glimpse of his hands. They are so plump and swollen as if they are riddled with arthritis. I wish he would just go to the doctor. We're not super low-income, but we live paycheck to paycheck. I would help, though the last time I worked an actual job, Adam freaked out on the manager, and he said that I needed to stay home.

I liked working. Although I enjoy my under-the-table work better. Sex sells, and it pays a hell of a lot more. I made just enough videos to fill up my nest egg. Could I ease the financial load? Yes, but Adam is so obsessed with money that I just can't guarantee that enough is ever enough for him. Plus, with how I made it, if he finds out, there is no way I would survive that fight. "So what are the plans today, babe?" He asks plainly.

"I'm headed to the bookshop. It's been a little bit since I've seen my best buddy." I beam. His eyes become empty and dark as he peers up from his food. I wonder if he can feel me slowly killing him or if he thinks it's exhaustion.

What is it with men not wanting to go to the doctor? I mean, the probability of the reason for all of his changes being caused by me is astronomically high. However, what if there is something more going on? What if I'm just speeding up the process of his inevitable demise? I wish he would let us open our relationship up. Nobody ever changed like Adam has and I'm really starting to get in my head about it.

Everyone I've ever loved has died. Why wouldn't Adam be next? "Your best buddy?" he grumbles, dropping his fork.

"Adam, please, you know I'm talking about Mr. M. That bookshop feels like home to me, and I couldn't imagine my life without him. He's been there for me ever since my mother disappeared." Mr. M's was one of the first places I stopped when I started hanging up the missing person fliers of my mom.

He insisted that I come back. He gave me a job. Taught me finances. Emphasized that a person can genuinely live once they mastered the Dewey Decimal system. He taught me how to be an adult and the joys of falling in love with literature.

"I don't care that he has been there for you since you were a kid, Lil. It isn't right that your best friend is a man, let alone one that is old enough to be your grandfather." Adam nearly yells. I swear my eye-roll is audible by the dark scowl he gives me. Here we go again. The old "you need more girlfriends and fewer dude friends" lecture. Followed by the "Why are you spending so much time at the bookstore? I do everything for you, so you don't have to work," argument.

Sometimes, I genuinely think that he wants me to be caged up in this house with no outside contact other than him. I am no princess, and I do not intend to be locked away in a tower any time soon. I gulp down my coffee quickly. The faster it's gone, the quicker I can get out of the house. Setting my untouched breakfast and the dirty cup into the sink guarantees my freedom. With a quick peck on his cheek, I haul ass out of the house before he can utter another word.

The moment I make it outside and down the block, I smell it: death. For me, the first signs of fall hit my nose before anything else. I know it has officially arrived when the world's fragrance is like this. I always get the brisk, sharp smell of rot.

I find it ironic how so many people fear death. Yet, nobody can get enough of its aroma when autumn comes around. Fall-scented candles, house fresheners, perfume, food, you name it, they have it.

The sound of wind rustling through the trees warms me. The leaves are just starting to lose their bright green color, which excites me even more. Before you know it, the city will become a beautiful masterpiece. Colors of all shades, the warm smell of chimney smoke, and fires lit in the neighbor's yards.

I wish it could stay this season all year. The clop of my boots is meditative as I take in the scenery of the city. Its kaleidoscope of colors and movement blur around me as people hurry along the sidewalks. Various shops and townhouses line the street like a patchwork quilt. Most standing tall with pride as they withstand the test of time with weathered bricks. As if my feet had a mind of their own, I find myself at the entrance of the best coffee shop in town.

Saint Drogo Roasters is by far my favorite place to stop in town, other than Mr. M's. My mouth waters at the sight of their pumpkin muffins. I can't research if my belly is empty. I still need to eat actual food, and warm, fluffy muffins are so much better than nasty eggs.

While opening the door, the familiar ring of the bells brings a warmth that washes over me. It's such a tiny shop, but they roast their coffee in-house with a roaster that is at least a hundred years old, and they make the best London Fog tea. Cramming into their narrow entry is worth it despite the claustrophobic feeling. The entire place is decorated in a way that feels like I stepped into a feel good holiday movie with knick knacks and family photos covering the walls. The dark green walls make everything inside pop.

"What can I get you, hun?" the barista chirps. I can't help myself eyeing up this cute blonde. Her dimples are nearly as adorable as her bright green doe eyes. Guys, girls, he, she, they, them, I don't really care. Unless they're a pretty girl, and this woman is gorgeous, which makes me nervous. It's a giggly sort of experience that warms my cheeks. I saw someone call it bi-panic, and honestly, so relatable.

"London Fog with soy, please." I order the same thing every time I come here. I have to have at least one a day. I catch her nibbling on her bottom lip as she scans me up and down with a broad smile. I rub the back of my neck, hoping it will bring me back from cloud nine. Her tiny chuckle as she turns away from the register warms me from the inside out. Damn it, she's adorable.

"One day, Lily, you might actually order something different. You do know we have seasonal drinks, right?" she jests from behind the counter. I pretend to read the seasonal menu above the food display, but what I'm hunting for is that muffin. The predator in me creeps in, reminding me that I'm not completely satisfied. We've been down this road before. She even asked me out a few times. I tried talking to Adam about opening up the relationship to her, and he quickly turned me down. So now we play this game of stolen glances. I love and hate it all at the same time.

"I'm going to stick with my usual order. However, this muffin…" There it is, that brightness that warms my heart. I point to the deep burnt orange muffin with sugar on top. She grabs the muffin and hands it to me forgoing a plate or brown bag. She knows I will eat right here in line as I wait on my tea. I groan at its moist, fluffy texture and hints of pumpkin. Perfectly balanced spices dance across my tongue with each bit. I put it on the counter halfway through and start digging through my bag, looking for my wallet. "This one is on me," a deep smooth voice says.

The warmth of a body curls around my side as a male hand lays a rectangular card on the counter. My skin ignites with heat as our bodies grow closer. Before I can check to see who is so close, his presence steals my attention away from my cute barista. Time slows, allowing my brain a split second to appreciate that this man's tan jacket perfectly complements his olive skin before it leaves me.

Slowly raking my eyes up his arm, the taste of sandalwood and red wine finds its way onto my palate, catching my breath and forcing me to hold on to my dignity for dear life. His sharp jawline and high cheekbone paint damn near perfect features, with wisps of honey hair falling forward.

As if that isn't enough, he takes his hidden hand, pushing the fallen strands out of his eyes. The world dissolves around me as his sky-blue eyes lock onto mine. For a moment, nothing but carnal *lust* exists between us. My breath becomes shallow and thready at the seductive grin his supple lips make.

"T-thank you, but that's not necessary. I can pay my own bill." Clearing my throat, I step back to get a full view of why my soul left its body.

"Oh, I have no doubt about it, but I didn't ask if you could," he admonished with a challenging tone. His mischievous smile wounds me to my core. The only thing I can feel is my heartbeat and the warmth growing between my legs. Challenge accepted, buddy. I force myself to lock eyes with him while firmly placing some cash on the counter for the barista to take.

"Do you make it a habit to piss people you just met off, or do you simply enjoy making an obnoxious appearance in stranger's lives unannounced?" I slide the cash closer to the barista. *Blip.* A long sigh of defeat leaves me as I glance at the register. He pulls his card away from the touch card reader. Sly fucker.

"I didn't think chivalry was considered obnoxious. I guess we can consider me educated then," he lightly chuckles. Damn it, this guy is good. I grab my tea and shove the rest of my muffin in my mouth. Clearly, I need to shut up, as I'm zero for two at this point. Now that I have made a complete ass of myself, there is only one thing left to do…run.

Moving my feet as fast as I can without actually running so I don't choke on the muffin, I book it out of Saint Drogo Roasters and head to Mr. M's. I can not let myself get involved with this guy.

Even if he has a perfectly chiseled jaw and is everything I have ever read about in a romance novel. I slow down to take a sip of my tea. The sweet vanilla with hints of bergamot citrus tantalizes my taste buds as it passes over my tongue, helping the last bit of food down my gullet. Next time, I'll enjoy the muffin. No more using food as a gag.

I mean, for real, what are these guys reading these days to think that would even butter me up to them? The audacity to pay for a girl's order when they obviously don't- "So where are we heading to?" A vaguely familiar deep voice scares me so bad that I can't hold back the blood-curdling scream escaping my throat.

"What the actual fuck, man! Why would you do that?!" I scold. The man actually starts belly laughing. Awesome. Even his laugh is charming. How aggravating. "Are you stalking me? Do you have a death wish?" He wipes his eye and pulls my cell phone out of his suit pocket. I had forgotten that thing's existence entirely. When did I even put that glorified bookmark down? Snatching it from his hand, I check to make sure it's really my phone.

"I don't know who Adam is, but he was not happy when I answered your phone. I tried to tell him I found it at the shop," he says through catching his breath. I can feel the shock growing on my face and my stomach hardens at the thought of this man answering a call from Adam. Nothing good can come from this.

"No, you didn't. Please tell me you're lying right now." Panic quickly replaces the feeling of being startled as my muffin threatens to reappear. I try to hold back the trembling as I stare at the call history. Adam did call. Son of bitch.

"I don't lie. I wasn't sure where you ran off to, so when it rang, I answered, figuring that would be the quickest way to return it to you." he replies nonchalantly. Deep breaths, Lily. Deep breaths. "Are you okay? You seem a little pale?" I can hear concern creeping into his tone.

I shove my phone back into my purse, finding a very concerned man with a single raised eyebrow taking a step towards me. Nervous and horny do not mix well, at least at this moment. "It's okay. I'm fine." I can handle this. "Thank you for bringing me my phone. How can I repay you?"

"How about a name?" he asks. This sexier than sin of a man reaches his hand towards me with a flirtatious cockeyed grin that awakens the butterflies in my stomach. "I'm Samael. You can call me Sam." he offers, his tone changing from concern to something more hopeful. I grab his hand, shaking it in a way that hopefully conveys that I am far from dainty and not attracted to him, even though I most definitely am.

"Lily. I want to say that it's been a pleasure to meet you, but this has already been a unique interaction, to say the least." I deadpan. We drop our handshake and Sam bites his bottom lip. This man is a force to be reckoned with. He needs to stop looking at me like I'm a whole ass meal.

"Seeing that Adam exudes a personality that I can only describe as resembling a sea cucumber, how about you call me when you finally realize you're worth a hell of a lot more than he has to offer?" he says while slowly walking backwards toward the road. A black car pulls up and parks right behind him. Without hesitation, Sam opens the door and gets into the back.

Before he closes the door, I yell to him, "And how do you expect me to do that without your number?" The car door slams shut, and he drives off. I bet he didn't think that through. What an idiot.

My phone rings with a picture of Sam popping up on the screen. I hope he can sense my annoyance as I answer. "You should put a password on that thing. You never know if some rando will add their number to your phone. Oh, and by the way, you should really stop making that face. It might freeze like that. I'll be waiting to hear from you." Before I can get a word out the call disconnects. Oh that was smooth.

3

Samael

I hang up the phone and settle into the sinfully smooth leather of my car. A wicked grin stretches across my face. The roar of the engine echoes the iniquitous anticipation building within me. I'm no stranger to the monsters that live on our streets. In contrast, a woman like Lily is a rare gem I have not yet had the pleasure of meeting.

"So, whose tree are you barking up this time? Anyone we gotta look out for?" Hal, my driver, is one of my most trusted employees. Not only does he drive me from place to place, but he also is my messenger and, through sheer luck, my longest-standing friend.

"No, she won't be trouble for us," I say while putting my phone away. Hal isn't a simple man, but for him to think Lily will be an issue of any sort is highly unlike him.

"Oh! I see it now! Right there on your smug face! You're smitten!" Hal belts out a laugh. I kick the back of his seat hard enough to shake him in his seat. He isn't wrong. I have never felt like this with anyone before. I'm not a person who enjoys the concept of relationships. The commitment thing isn't my style. Though this woman makes me reconsider my life choices. There is something about her that draws me in. Lily is just as beautiful as she is snarky. The faint blue flame that flickers in her eyes is so unique. I have to know what she is.

"You watch your mouth. Smitten is different from what's going on here." I snap back, my harsh tone at odds with the smile on my face. "Infatuation, eh. Maybe possessiveness. Now, obsession, absolutely," I muse aloud drawing out the last word painfully long. Hal is that brother that I never knew I needed. Always ready to remind me that I'm not always as intimidating as I portray myself.

"Well, I hate to be the bearer of bad news, but you need to get your head in the game, Sam. This guy is a real piece of work, and if you fuck this up, may I remind you, we are missing out." Hal's tone is more serious. He's right. This client is truly perfect.

I grab the case file Hal hands to me and start reading. Thoughts of manipulating the legal dance swirl in my mind like a malevolent waltz with each step leading me closer to the courtroom's infernal embrace. Leaning back, I methodically sift through the paperwork in my client's file.

The weight of responsibility hangs in the air as I delve into the intricacies of the case once more to prepare for battle. With a final dissection, I comb through fallible witness statements and arbitrary evidence I can easily manipulate in our favor. Each page is a puzzle piece, fitting together wonderfully to form a flawless defense strategy that will free my client from the system. Allowing me to bind him to my services for the foreseeable future. Blackmail is such a glorious thing when used appropriately.

As soon as this case came across my desk, I knew he was perfect. Cain Jubilee is a man of simple upbringing. His parents own a farm where they grew and raised damn near everything. When he was twenty-three, he was arrested for the murder of his brother. According to the court documents, Cain and Abel worked in the fields preparing for harvest that day.

His mother, Eve, testified that the brothers were not on amicable terms for the last few months and that she and their father decided that it would be best for them to work together in hopes that they figured their shit out. The next thing they knew, they found Cain holding onto his dead brother's body, covered in blood. The weapon of choice was a fucking rock.

It was lucky for Cain to have a fantastic lawyer at the time. That son of a bitch got him off over the fact that there were also puncture marks on Abel Jubilee's neck. The coroner's report stated that those puncture wounds sat right on top of an artery and couldn't be distinguished between a post- or perimortem injury.

His lawyer led with the defense that Cain was attempting to save his brother from an animal attack. I wish I could meet that man to shake his hand. Every bit of evidence showed that Cain was guilty on all accounts, and somehow that silver-tongued snake found a way to convince the jury of his bullshit. He either selected the perfect jury or paid off the coroner to lie on his report. After that beautiful trial, Cain left town. He was never seen nor mentioned again until now and, once again, there is a body involved.

This time, the case is more straightforward than his first. Three weeks ago, some punk named Gabriel came running into the police station screaming that he had proof of a murder. They said he had passed out when he reached the intake desk. It took three days for him to wake up. Apparently, this guy was waiting for his order at a late-night pop-up event when he was startled by a woman screaming.

Gabriel followed the screams to an alleyway. As he got there, the screaming stopped, and instead, he heard what was described as the sound of something eating. Gabriel said he started to record on his phone, walked toward the noise, and claimed that there was a man roughly fitting the description of Cain on top of the victim's body eating her. The police went back to the location of the crime scene. They found a woman, who was later identified as Cain's sister, Awan Jubilee, dead. The coroner listed the cause of death as exsanguination.

I'm no cartographer, but this sure as hell isn't Florida. As far as I'm aware, there aren't any new drugs floating around that will make someone eat another person. Detective Azrael can't even come up with a theory on how a woman would be drained of all of her blood without having a single puncture wound or signs of internal bleeding. The thought of having Azrael on the witness stand trying to explain this has me foaming at the mouth.

Azrael is one of Michael's, as he likes to call them, Heavenly Corps. Pretentious ass. Each member of Michael's team has something more about them, just like my team but on the complete opposite side of the spectrum. Where I make it my business to find unique individuals who are more than capable, Michael collects those who are all righteous.

"Hey, boss, we're here," Hal says, breaking my concentration on the case. I nod to him and close my case file, shoving it into my briefcase. The courthouse materializes before me, the stage where I wield my legal prowess with devilish charm, defending the scum of the Earth, striking a diabolical bargain with the very concept of corruptible justice. Hal hops out and opens my door after he stops the car at the drop-off zone.

"This may take a couple of hours. I have to meet with the client before we get in there. I'll text you when we are finished. In the meantime, I need you to run a full background check on that woman." I quickly send him her contact profile and wait for the ding that lets me know he got it. "I want to know everything. Where she lives, her daily habits, the people she associates with, the entire work up."

"When you fall, you fall hard. I'll get Levi on this. He's talented at all that techy stuff." Hal chuckles as he pulls out his phone. He shows me that he got the contact link I sent him and closes my car door, then heads back to the driver's side.

"I mean it. I want everything on her by the time I leave this building. She's unique in more than one way." Hal nods in acknowledgment, and hops back into the car, driving off, leaving me just enough time to get my game face on.

This morning, the capital office is packed with lawyers, witnesses, and observers in the endless rat race.

As chaos surges around me, I consume it as if it is my last meal. The fear and pride spilling from each person is more than filling. Marble tile and bright lights amplify my path to success as I make my way further in. "Judge Michael wants to see you in his chambers before the hearing, Samael." With a nod, I gather my things from the security table and follow the guard. The sound of our steps is lost among the loud building. People chat in the hallway, some point to various paintings hung, while others are simply just trying to get where they need to go.

They must be trying for a life sentence with Judge Michael on this. Meeting with Cain should be the priority. Being ushered into the judge's chambers, an unsettling agitation takes hold. The inconvenience of this pre-trial exchange gnaws at me, forcing me to hold my tongue. Michael knows he's disrupting the rhythm of my preparations. It's a clear display of the imaginative power he thinks he has over me.

I yearn to plunge into the courtroom, yet here I am, compelled to navigate the monotonous waters of judicial dialogue before the trial begins. The sound of his chamber doors opening pulls me from ruminating on all the different ways I would like to make him suffer.

"Thank you for meeting me, Samael. I realize this is inconvenient, and I won't take up much of your time," Michael says as he walks to his closet, grabbing the official black robe to put on. Michael is only an inch or two taller than me, with light brown hair, and a face you just want to punch because it's just that pretty. Asshole. Just by the way his grey suit fits tight around his arms, I bet he's a fitness freak now too.

"What do you want, Mikey? You know I have to brief my client before we get in there," I snap. The power between us reverberates through the room as if the battle of good and evil is between us and only us.

"We need to talk about the trial. I already spoke with opposing counsel about the matter. It is inherently obvious that the media has taken a liking to this case and wants to cover it. As you know, this is a public space, and I cannot close it off," he says. Michael opens his desk drawer and pushes a piece of paper toward me.

"The media has expressed a distinct interest in this since the original recording of the incident hit social media and have requested to cover the case for live television. I don't see a reason to deny them. I need you and your client to sign these, allowing them to record and air the trial. It's just a formality, I'm sure you understand." Michael remains stoic and cocky as ever.

Fuck, how am I supposed to make sure Cain acts the part? This good for nothing bastard knew this was going to happen weeks in advance, at the very least. "That shouldn't be an issue. Is there anything else, or were you just hoping to catch my dick in my hand?"

Michael pauses for a moment. "No, that's all," he says, waving me out of his office.

* * *

Rubbing my face, I make my way into the conference room. Cain is already here with his head laying on the large table in the center of the room. By the look of it, the taxpayers' money went to shit use with these renovations. The tacky blue rug feels cheap under my Italian leather dress shoes. I hate this. Clearly, they didn't actually care much, seeing that they didn't even spring for a real wood table. I can see the seam where the plastic overlay is pretending not to cover up the particle board underneath. Before laying my briefcase onto the table, I gently squeeze one of the ten chairs. Just what I thought, pleather.

"Alright, listen up, shithead. This is going to be an easy win." I set my briefcase on the table between us. "If you do exactly what I say, then there is no reason you won't be freed and clear. Tell me again what I told you." Cain's dark copper, hollow eyes are that of something vile. His thin muscular frame smoothly curls up as he gives me his full attention. Strands of black hair curl slightly down to the top of his cheeks, contrasting his pale complexion and accentuating a malevolence he seems to be making no attempt to conceal.

I can use his immense dog energy outside these walls, but he needs to calm down. If the jury feels threatened by him, it only makes it much more difficult to sell his innocence. I need a cinnamon roll, not this.

"Keep my mouth shut and pretend that I'm innocent," Cain clears his throat, "If I don't, you'll try to kill me yourself." Cain smiles and I catch a glimpse of his sharp canines. *Crack!* A light pink impression of my hand forms on his cheek.

Composing myself from the much needed violent therapy, I grab tight to his jumper and drop my voice. "I won't have to try. I own you. You may be getting off for murder since these idiots can't tell the difference between their head and their asshole. So, when we finish the trial, you work directly for me. Do you understand?" I'm seething at this point. Though I know better than to let it get the best of me. In my peripheral I can see a red mark hanging just below his ear. Fuck.

Cain doesn't move. He isn't even giving me an ounce of eye contact. It's as if he is stuck in a trance, fixated on my neck. "I'm sorry," I chuckle. "it appears that you believe you have a choice in this matter. I'm going to ask you one more time. DO. YOU. UNDERSTAND?" Cain softens his eyes and finally looks at me.

"Yes." Cain says through gritted teeth. I drop my hands and fix my jacket, returning it to the more professional uniformity of the courtroom.

"I have a job lined up for you; you'll need your strength. So, do whatever you need to do to get that in order. I employ monsters, not petty criminals." I shift through my briefcase to grab the papers Michael gave me.

"One last thing," Cain huffs, and I give him a glare to convey my disapproval. He will learn how to act sooner or later. For his sake, it better be sooner. "The judge gave me these documents for us to sign. The video they are using against you has gone viral, and now the media wants to use this case for live television. You need to sign this." I put them on the desk.

Scratching my signature on the papers quickly, I flip the papers around and slide them towards Cain and place my pen on top of them. When he takes it, his fingers graze mine. His hands feel like they have touched death. "Shit, do you need a jacket or something? You're freezing."

Cain signs the papers and pushes them and the pen back toward me. "No, I'm fine. I run cold. It doesn't even faze me anymore," he chuckles.

4

Samael

S tepping into the courtroom, an air of confidence envelopes me like a well-tailored suit. The room gives the impression of it bowing to my presence with its polished mahogany and imposing bench. The gentle hum of whispered conversations is louder than usual as the media takes up most of the room filling it and nervous shuffling of papers from the prosecution prelude to the performance waiting to unfold. Cain is brought in by a less than enthused bailiff and seated next to me. He better shut the fuck up like we discussed.

The longer I can keep him from being called to the witness stand, the better. Thankfully, this is going to be a lengthy proceeding. The prosecutor will want to question him, but the number of witnesses I threw in there should buy me some time. "All rise for Judge Michael," the bailiff booms.

The court stands in unison, waiting for his permission to sit down. Michael ascends to his podium, and the light bends, creating a halo around him as if he has a white light of protection shrouded around him. The showboater just can't resist wasting time taking a slow walk to his podium. When he is finally through mindlessly shuffling the papers up there, Michael has us all sit.

"Thank you, ladies and gentlemen, for coming here today. I expect everyone who is here to be on their best behavior. These proceedings will be long and trying. However, we must fully understand this case so the jury can decide objectively. I will not hesitate to kick you out of my courtroom if you speak out of turn or cause a commotion. The trial is The State vs Cain Jubilee. How do you plead?" Michael waits for our response. I glare at Cain to keep his mouth shut.

In unison, Cain and I stand. "My client pleads Not Guilty, your Honor," I proclaim. Michael stares at me in a way that gets me all tingly inside. I indulge in a small smile over the fact that I can aggravate that man with just my presence.

"Very well then. We will start in the usual order. If the prosecution will please start the opening statements." Michael waves his hand towards them as Cain and I retake our seats.

The representative for the state turns a shade of green. This must be her first recorded case. It isn't often we have to put on a show. The back of the courtroom is wholly filled with cameras and reporters. The continuous flashes reflecting off the walls can easily distract anyone.

She isn't ready for this. The prosecution moves shakily in front of the jury. She spends at least thirty minutes explaining why my client is guilty—outlining every detail, telling them a lovely story about how righteous of a person the victim was, and making an unprofessional spectacle of herself with several pauses throughout her statement. I knew she would get distracted. When she sits down, she takes a long breath. Don't worry, baby girl. I'll show you exactly how this is done.

I stand up and re-button my suit jacket. Smoothing out any creases. As I step out into the aisle between us, I glance over at the opposing counsel, giving her a wink. Her expression of feigned confidence melts away.

With legal briefs, I approach the podium in front of the jury with a stride that conveys assurance and poise. What a miserable bunch. Michael stares me down, and I acknowledge his presence with a subtle nod, aware that every eye and camera in the room is on me.

"Ladies and gentlemen of the jury, today I stand before you as the defense counsel entrusted with the solemn duty of advocating for my client. I won't take as much time as the opposing counsel here." I take a deep breath and push my authoritative energy forward to the jury as a subtle reminder of who will pay them after this. "As riveting as her tale is, the rules of this courtroom are clear."

Stepping down from the podium I move closer to the jury. "They state that the prosecution's job is to prove to you that my client is guilty beyond reasonable doubt. I am here to tell you that this is entirely impossible. This case has more reasonable doubt than I have ever witnessed in my career. There is no weapon to be mentioned in the evidence. The investigation team could not locate a single drop of blood or scrap of DNA at the crime scene." Raising my voice at the end to make sure they get the point.

"Most importantly, we are now wasting our time and tax dollars to put an innocent man on trial for a crime he did not commit. Awan is now the second and final sibling of Cain Jubilee, whom he has been forced to bury well before their time and stand trial unjustly for false allegations against him," I yell and point to Cain. A tear falls from his eye. Now that is some good acting.

I make my way over to Cain and give him a tissue from the table he sits at, making it appoint to soften my tone to something more sullen and somber. "Once again, my client sits here in court, accused of the murder of a sibling. Poor Abel died in an animal attack, and now his sister, whose cause of death isn't fully understood nor explainable." I turn to the jury. "Not a single medical professional can explain how this young woman had lost every last drop of blood in her body. There are no weapons. There are no visibly sustained injuries. The cause of death is even listed on the coroner's report as idiopathic hemorrhaging. Which can be translated from fancy medical terminology as they don't know." I make my way back to the podium, gripping the sides of it softly with both hands.

"As we embark on this legal journey, I urge you to weigh the evidence presented and the nuances that shape the narrative against my client. I trust you will also see the holes in the prosecution's argument and come to a sensible outcome, just as I have. In the pursuit of justice, let us navigate the intricate paths of truth, seeking clarity amidst the shadows of uncertainty. Thank you." I can sense panic rising in the prosecution. Their suffering brings me so much pleasure I can hardly resist eating it up.

* * *

Leaving the building is chaos: cameras, flashes, interviewers screaming for me to tell them anything. The mass pandemonium this case has already caused will be the death of me if they don't calm down.

Fighting through the crowd would be much more difficult

if Hal and the police weren't here to bat them off. A plethora of voices surround me. "How do you feel about the case thus far? Will you be putting Cain on the stand? When you said that this case has the most reasonable doubt you have ever seen, what exactly do you mean? What are your opinions on the prosecution? Sir! Sir! SIR!"

The mad screams of these piranhas follow me to the car. Hal struggles to open the door as they surround us. "BACK OFF YOU BLOODY LEECHES!" Hal's unique northern accent finds its way to the surface. He is pissed, and for good reason. Fighting them off isn't going to work.

Standing between the car door and my seat, I face them. "Listen, everyone, I am only going to say this once, and you all better listen up." I project my voice. The crowd silences with only the sound of cameras capturing photos to break it.

"The case will be outlined completely within the trial. I will not be taking any questions, nor will my client. It is my job to defend my client and prove his innocence. That is exactly what I intend to do." With swift movements, I get into the car and shut the door. "Get me the fuck out of this circus, Hal," I groan.

Hal accelerates promptly, squealing the tires and leaving the reporters in a cloud of smoke. After a few moments of silence and a heavy sigh escaping my lips, a manila envelope sitting next to me catches my attention. "Is this what I asked for?" I ask. Hal cautiously nods from the driver's seat, wasting no time.

"Levi found everything he could on her, but it wasn't easy, I can tell you that much. Let's just say that the boys and I contributed a little to the cause." Hal's accent is still there on the edge of his words. He's still flustered. I don't blame him. That was excessive. I grab the envelope and open it. As I shuffle through the papers, I see what they mean.

"How many did you watch?" I inquire through gritted teeth. Hal clears his throat, and his eyes dart back and forth between the rearview mirror and the road.

"Only a couple, Sammy. I gotta say that one is quite bendy. She made this one video with a dildo that had multiple tentacles, and she-" Hal looks back and immediately stops talking. My jaw tightens as I clench it. Hal peeks back at me through the rearview mirror, and his eyes flit back and forth. He clears his throat. "You're going to have a lovely time with her. She's a true virtuoso if you ask me." he notes nervously. Snapshots of Lily consume nearly half the fucking file.

"And I have all the pictures the boys tried to keep for themselves, correct?" I say it more as a statement than a question. I better have all the pictures. As we stop at the red light, Hal places his hand on the back of the passenger seat twisting his body closer.

"As I sit here and breathe, you have all the pictures I found Levi printed off before I left." Hal raises his hand to the sky. "On my mother, God rest her soul." Hal turns back around and starts to drive again.

Name: Lily Isaiah **Sex:** Female **Alias:** Unknown
DOB: 06/25/1992 Age:32 **Occupation:** Self-employed
Marriage Status: Single
Father: Unknown
Mother: Deceased
Siblings: Sister- Deceased
Active Associations: Adam Genesis, Benjamin Mephisto
Cellular Data analysis: Frequently visited locations in the

last thirty days include current residence, Saint Drogo Rosters, Mr. M's Bookshop Vintage Volumes & Antiques

The more I read, the more confused I become. Why would Lily restrict herself to so few places and people? She isn't married. She has more money than she needs to have a luxurious life. Knowing my men, I can guarantee it. Regardless, I understand wanting to live a simple life, but this is extreme.

I replay the morning with her in my head. Every detail from her mannerisms, her expressions, her long chestnut hair, how her amorous brown doe eyes focused so skillfully on my lips, the smell of her jasmine and vanilla perfume, the demanding energy she gives off that pulls me in.

Her full crimson-painted lips and how heavenly they would look wrapped around my cock. I want her in every depraved way possible. I want to hear her whimper as I wrap her hair around my hand. Gagging her until tears stream down her beautiful porcelain skin, running streaks of black that outline her rosy cheeks. Filling her with all my desire only to lay her down and worship her pussy.

I can feel the undertones of rage bubble inside of me. Lily clearly isn't too happy that I answered the phone and spoke with the sea cucumber. She borderline panicked after telling her. Her behavior was reluctant and fidgety.

Fury ignites my darkened soul as the realization hits. I may be many depraved things, but I am not like him. If he is doing what I think he is, then I need to tread very carefully. I need to gain her trust first. That is the only way this will work. I will ensure there is a truly horrifying place in hell for men like Adam. "Uhh, boss? You okay?" Hal interrupts my train of thought for the second time today.

"Get me everything on Adam Genesis," I growl.

5

Lily

I don't know what else to do. I've called Adam so many times already. His phone just keeps going to voicemail. Texts are being left on read. The park is only a short walk away from Mr. M's. I can just go home, but what good will that do?

A gentle breeze passes through my hair. With a deep cleansing breath, I settle into the bench at the park. Instead of focusing on Adam, I choose to hone in on my surroundings to relax this feeling of impending doom. Taking in a few more steady breaths, I stand up and make my way to Mr. M.

The bird's melodious tune is hardly deafened by the distant bustle of city life. Leaves rustle with a sound that resembles crinkling paper. The sunlight gently kisses away the chill from my skin, bringing me back to the present. Mindfulness has become a regular practice for me. It's the only thing that I have found that can keep me steady when my mind begins to race.

I swear, I can sense Mr. M's Bookshop from a block away.

When I discovered Mr. M's Bookshop for the first time as a teenager, I wholeheartedly believed I had found a portal to the past. As I get closer, those old feelings bubble up.

Ivy covers the aged bricks underneath the ancient structure, smelling of earth and impossible fantasies. Each slight gust of wind coaxes the creaky wooden sign to wave at people like a bell calling in those worthy of the knowledge that dwells just behind its heavy door.

A bibliophile's wildest dreams could come true here. The painted golden lettering on the glass window gleams, filling me with possibilities as the fireplace within promises warmth. Having a fireplace in a bookshop is quite strange, but Mr. M insists on maintaining the history behind these walls.

Walking into the bookshop eases my mind and soul more than any meditative practice can. The day's chaos falls away with the cracking of firewood and the smell of aged vanilla. The stumpy old man could always be found sitting in his reading chair among what he calls his life's passion, sipping home-brewed tea and forever reading.

Mr. M's grey eyes twinkle in the light as he peeks up from his book, with bells ringing behind me announcing my return, resembling that of a thin Santa Claus with his bald head and bushy white beard. He's wearing a variation of his everyday business attire: khaki pants, a long sleeved white shirt, and a dark green knitted sweater vest. His tiny bifocals rest near the tip of his nose, dawning a smile that isn't just inviting but loving.

"Lily, my dear, I was wondering when you would come." The euphonious sound of his voice is gentle and nostalgic to my ears. I take my jacket and hat off, carefully placing it on the coat rack that just may be as old as the building itself.

"I'm sorry, Adam has been a little... difficult lately, but I promise to start coming more often soon." I respond with an apologetic shrug and what I hope is a placating smile. The sturdy reading chair creaks from his weight as he shifts his body towards me, placing his bifocals into his sweater pocket. The face he makes is one I can only imagine an understanding father would provide.

"You know I never did like that boy. If you had asked me for my opinion, I would say he isn't part of your story. The best parts of your story that is," he clarifies with a forced smile. Despite the age painted across his face, Mr. M places his book down and smoothly rises from the chair.

"Lily, I will never tell you what to do, but I must warn you. Nothing positive is going to come from continuing down this path. This story was written long before you were even a thought. I've read it enough times that I can see the signs. The last thing I wish to see is you get hurt. When and if you choose to abandon this discomforting affiliation, I have a place for you in the shop. You're no Myrtle Wilson," Mr. M says lovingly.

He moves closer to me and pats the shelf, passing his fingers across his prized collection of tales on his way over. "Enough of that now, my dear. How about a cup of tea?" he asks without turning around.

Mr. M moves through the shop with prideful confidence. I can never repay him for the kindness he has shown me throughout my life. Prom dress shopping, showing up to graduation, helping me pay for college, advice, life lessons, care, openness, the list is equally priceless as it is endless.

He's always there for me, even when I don't think I need him to be. Coming back into the shop after months of absences is magical. I want to keep from romanticizing this moment, but so many memories are etched into these floorboards.

The secrets they have heard me tell, the tears they have caught, are almost overwhelming. I hate that Adam has kept me away for so much time. Though I can't blame him entirely. I'm the one who chose to listen to his demands of visiting less. Regret coils its thieving thorns around my roots.

Wandering through the narrow aisles, I can't help but feel the weight of nostalgia settle around me, dimming the lament of lost time. The scent of aged paper and ink triggers a flood of memories, as if each book is a vessel carrying me back to the days of yesteryears.

My fingers trace the spines, a habit I picked up from Mr. M, unlocking chapters of my past. Losing myself to the echoes of the young woman I once was, who once reveled in the enchantment of these shelves. This bookshop is more of a home to me than anywhere else. Each volume, softly worn and aged under my fingers with the comforting sound of a light *thwap,* calling to memories long ignored.

I vividly recall the day I first saw an ancient text in this shop. I had told my aunt about being bisexual, and she shot me down, telling me how I was sick and that I was an ungodly creature living in sin and needing salvation. The sting of her words cut me so deeply that I ran here. Mr. M found me sitting in the back of the shop with a tear-stained face. He dragged my chair to the fireplace with me still seated in it and brought me a hot cup of tea.

When I finally settled, he coaxed my emotions forth with gentle words of understanding. Through his assurance of non-judgment, I told him about how there was this girl I really liked and how I also liked a couple of boys in my grade as well. He kept true to his promise.

Instead of following the path of my aunt, he told me that it was nothing to be ashamed of. Mr. M explained to me that there are some people in the world who refuse to see past the tip of their noses, and it can form them into a tainted vessel fueled with malicious intent. It was at that moment a silent pact was made between us. He became my mentor, and I offered up my unwavering trust.

I stayed for some time that day, helping around the shop just to avoid going home. As I browsed the shelves, a thick weathered tome caught my attention, its cracked leather binding and deeply tanned pages a testament to the centuries that it had passed. At that moment, time seemed to stand still. Whispers of unholy matrons shrouded me in unison, beckoning me to reach out for it.

Restraint disappeared as I carefully lifted the ancient text, feeling the weight of its history in my hands. The fragrance of aged parchment filled the air while delicately opening it, curiosity compelling me to discover a world long gone and words unknown to me.

With each page, a vicious symphony of melodic hymns encapsulated my attention, drawing my mind further into the depth of consecration. Dragging me deeper into the harmonious darkness of my soul, forcing the hunger I now know to claw its way from my very being into the present. As the memory unfolds, my skin vibrates with anticipation, reminding me of my curse and its damnation.

My life changed entirely that day. Once simple desires to be forevermore led by unrelenting hunger solely for its survival, tearing away all the satisfaction life has to offer. Before opening the book, I was invisible. Unseen by wandering eyes, a fly on the wall. Since then, I was reborn into a coveted trophy. A nefarious malediction calling to those consumed by fornication in all ways. Men and women alike flock lustfully to an unspoken promise I did not intend to make.

Each pleading for a moment of my attention and the opportunity to lay in my bed. Once the initial discomfort faded, I became lost in the unrivaled attention I had to offer. I was determined to hone my skills of seduction: practicing poses, fine tuning my appearance, and even developing mannerisms that would secure my position as, for all intents and purposes, a lolita. The world was mine for the taking, and I ate my fill. The moment I became an adult, I knew how I could make my money. Living a life as a lady of the night allowed me to satiate the ravenousness of my affliction.

Though, as many things do, that path faded into an echo as the dangers of that world became more perilous. Finding my way into a polycule was cleaner and safer than selling myself on the corner. There was no more fear of contracting a venereal disease from random strangers off the street. The money I had saved over that time began to fade. So, I produced videos instead, and that paid quite well.

Despite stopping making videos after Adam and I went off alone, I still get regular checks. Thank you direct deposit. I'm not ashamed of what I was. It's what I have become that has me riddled with fear. How long can I go on the scraps that Adam provides me until I consume him whole?

I'm smacked with the reality of where and when I am as Mr. M walks into the room with a tray. "Tea time is the best time because tea time is some me time!" he sings. I will never tire of his little tunes.

Shaking the memories away, I cheerfully reply, "When it's me time during the tea time, I sing this little tune!" The smile of this old fool warms me up. Taking my glass from the tray, the perfumed steam of beautiful floral oolong curls up. "I've missed you so much, M. I promise I'm going to be around more often again. Maybe I can even help you around the store like old times." Mr. M chuckles. His glossy eyes are framed with wrinkles and age.

"I would like that very much, my dear." he answers, his gruff voice full of emotion. Our shared memories unfold like well-loved novels as we reminisce, binding us to our friendship's warmth. We spend much of the day catching up, discussing his impressive collection's newest additions. Talking about Adam and how our relationship is going. As customers come in, I take those opportunities to feel useful. Searching for new titles and rediscovering old ones as well. Helping people and giving Mr. M a much-deserved break from his daily tasks, and me time away from the monotony of life that I desperately need.

With dusk creeping into the world, the fireplace's flames grow brighter. The crackling warmth of the fire envelops me, casting a cozy glow that dances on the walls. The aroma of burning wood mingles with the crisp autumn air that creeps in with the day's foot traffic, creating a comforting ambiance that soothes the soul as I relax into my chair, next to my best friend, with a book and some peppermint tea to share.

Immersing the fading day within the bookshop's charm, the transition to night unfolds gracefully. Electric candles scattered throughout the store spontaneously ignite, casting a soft radiance on the well-worn volumes and aged wooden shelves.

It feels like the stories keep us company, their whispers echoing through the familiar aisles of my younger years. If I had to pick out a perfect day, this would be it. The final drops of tea find their way down my throat, "I have to head home. It's getting late, and I'm sure Adam is waiting for me," I announce, completely failing to hide my disappointment. I start cleaning up our mess, and as I take Mr. M's cup, he gently grasps my hand.

"Are you sure you're going to be okay walking home by yourself? Do you want me to call you a cab?" he asks. The concern in his eyes is amplified by the whips of flames reflecting off his face.

"And miss out on the opportunity to enjoy this beautiful night? You know me better than that." Mr. M gets up from his seat and gives me a tight squeeze then walks me out the door locking up for the night as I leave.

6

Samael

A neon-lit façade looms ahead as Hal drives us closer to the front door of Dragon's Hoard Casino. People from all walks of life flock towards the gleaming beacon of excitement and false promises. Hal opens my door with a nod, and the hum of activity surrounds me. As I step onto the red carpet, fresh sin brushes my lips, ready for me to consume it.

"Park the car and have some fun," I instruct. Pulling some cash out of my wallet, I hand it to Hal. He deserves a night off, and this is the one place where I can do my business without pesky interference. The distant chime of slot machines grows louder as the automatic doors swoosh open, welcoming me into the pulsating heart of this den of greed. Hal smiles broadly and rushes to the driver's seat, leaving me to my devices.

Entering the bustling casino, a symphony of slot machines jingle and distant cheers envelop me. The vibrant lights dance off polished surfaces, creating a kaleidoscope of colors. The air, thick with cigarette smoke and anticipation, tickles my throat as players of all types focus on cards and dice. All of them chasing fleeting fortunes within the lively chaos. The occasional roulette spin adds a rhythmic hum to the atmosphere, beckoning me towards it.

I approach the roulette table with a stack of saved chips in hand. They call it the Devil's Game, and I have yet to lose. The smooth surface, adorned with numbers and colors, beckons as I place my bet with a cunning gesture onto my guess. The croupier releases the ivory ball onto the spinning wheel, as time slows its movements while I carefully track its journey.

"No more bets," the croupier announces to the table. The clatter of the ball on the frets echoes suspensefully. As the wheel halts, exhilaration and uncertainty fill the air. The fate of my chips lies on the numbered slot where the ball comes to rest, and for a moment, the casino world revolves around that spinning wheel. The croupier carefully studies the table, "Red-six." He collects the chips across the board and pushes my winnings towards me. "Congratulations, Sir," he says.

I stay in my seat, reveling in the waves of emotion that flood this small corner of the world. With every win repeatedly, I place the entirety of my winnings on my guess, only to have the croupier clear the table of them, pushing the sum to me. With the energy ramping up, I relish the sharp acidic flavor of each person's corruption as it slides across my tongue. A boundless feast fit for me.

It's only a matter of time before my meal is interrupted by a firm hand squeezing my shoulder and a deep voice whispering, "Mr. Tatsu has requested your audience in his office." I haphazardly gather up my winnings and suck in a final tasting of this delectable meal. The croupier stares eagerly, adding a savory finish to my feast. His hands jut out as I flip the croupier a black one-hundred-dollar chip.

"Thanks for the game." The kid snatches it out of the air, placing it in his pocket with a beaming smile. The Dragon's Hoard isn't somewhere I particularly enjoy being just from the smell of sweat and desperation among many other things, so the interruption is well-timed.

Two men in clean black suits show me to the office and open the ornate door, allowing me to enter the den. The larger of the security team steps into the room behind me. I would invite this man home with me tonight if this was anything other than a business meeting. His hands appear soft and robust, and the outline of that python he fails to hide in his pants would make for one hell of a good time. Pressure builds, restricting the little room I have in my pants. I wanted to be both comfortable and stylish so I opted for my dark grey skinny dress pants and a semi-casual white button up, but now I am seriously regretting my choices.

"He will be with you in just a moment, sir. Mr. Tatsu says to make yourself comfortable and enjoy the beverages provided at his bar." The security guard folds his arms in front of him. I walk up to him and give the man a black chip.

"Are you included with that offer?" I slip the chip into his pants pocket when he doesn't take it. The man's eyes widen, and he quickly leaves, closing the door behind him. "I guess not." I sigh before running my fingers through my hair as I turn away from the door. Too bad, we could have had a lot of fun together.

The luxury of this space is immediately apparent when fully stepping into the office. Rich dracaena furnishings perfume the air with their distinct amber scent. At the same time, an oversized carved desk commands attention at the center of the room. Wall-to-wall windows reveal a panoramic view of the bustling casino floor below. Adorned with framed awards and scattered gemstones, the room is a testament to Mr. Tatsu's success in the industry. Soft ambient lighting casts a warm glow, creating an atmosphere that blends business prowess with the glamour of this imaginative world.

Behind the expansive desk, a discreet door opens to reveal a personal bar haven. The shelves are organized with an impressive collection of rare spirits and aged scotch, each bottle telling its own story. The polished dracaena bar gleams and the soft glow of under-cabinet lighting sets a relaxed mood. I grab a crystal glass and help myself to some Macallan Adami 1926. The amber liquid coats my mouth with hints of cherry and sweet oak. One can only imagine how he obtained the most expensive bottle of scotch known to man. The door clicks open behind me.

"Ah, I see you have found my newest collection piece. It cost me $2.7 million for that one." The tall man steps into the room. His wrist is adorned with a gold watch. Golden coins trail down the front of his dark blue well-tailored suit, filling the space where practical buttons would generally lay.

"What do you think of it?" he probes as he closes the door behind him and walks closer to me. I swirl the liquid in my glass and pull a mouthful in. Taking my time, I move the fluid around my mouth while venting the alcohol through pursed lips. With the final swallow, I smack my lips a few times to grow the anticipation.

"I would have paid three million for it, honestly. As usual, you have outdone yourself," I declare while lifting the glass in a half toast. A broad smile grows across Manny's face as he steps in front of me. In unison, our arms widen, and we embrace each other in a quick, friendly hug.

"I'm sorry you had to come here. I've got a few things going on here that require my attention, old friend. What can I help you with?" Manny pours himself a glass and motions for us to sit on the couches in the room. Manny is one of the most intelligent individuals I know in this business. He was on trial for money laundering after I first left my father's business and I represented him.

The evidence against Manny was compelling, but I was able to find one little flaw to get him off free and clear. Manny never deals with transactions in person, so they never had him on camera. All they had were witnesses stating that he was their boss. Of course, he was, in fact, their boss since they were all employed here at the casino.

"There is a case I am working on, and I need my client on the roster. His name is Cain Jubilee. Right now, he is on trial for the murder of his sister. I don't doubt that he did it, but the evidence is circumstantial. This kid is one of us, and having him on our side will benefit the company." Cain is going to be a useful asset to the team. With his abilities, depending on how developed they are, he will make a great soldier. I will need more of them when it's time to make our move against the Heavenly Corps.

"In the long term, I hope we can get to his previous employer and bring them into our team using him." I do my best to act as casual and professional as possible. We are both busy men. It's best to lead with what this meeting is about rather than mincing words. Time is money with Manny, and although he would silently suffer through wasting time talking about the weather, his temper would likely find it impertinent.

Manny takes a long sip of his drink and pulls a cigar from

the Gurkha Black Dragon box before him. "I see. So what exactly does this, Cain, have to offer? Adding another person to the books is within the budget, but what is his skill set?" Manny lights the cigar and puffs thick smoke rings from his lips. "We have plenty of soldiers. We don't exactly need any more of them." Now the hard part. I square my shoulders slightly and walk over to the couch across from him.

Leaning back onto the leather couch, I stretch out my arms. "Yes, but how many of them are relatively untraceable?" I cock my head to the side and cross my legs. Manny makes no reaction to my question as he ashes his cigar into the tall ashtray beside him.

"None. We lost our last ghost. What has it been now? Three years?" I nod in agreement.

"Exactly. Cain shows similar skills to her and the same type of…" I clear my throat "Motivation. The payment, I suspect, will be similar as well." I take another pull of my drink. Hints of vanilla and toffee coat my tongue, going down with the slightest of burns. Damn, this is a delicious scotch.

"Are you confident he is the same as her, or are we playing a cute guessing game like a couple of children? She was the best, and so few of her kind are left." he says with a frown. Manny's doubt is not surprising since she has been missing for quite some time. My gaze dips to my glass as I measure my response carefully. Noticing so little left of the scotch, I motion to the bar.

"Do you mind if I top off my glass?" Manny nods. Walking to the bar, I make it a point to remain silent. I pop the cork and pour myself two fingers' worth. I swirl the scotch in my glass to let it breathe while Manny shifts uncomfortably. "I think she started recruiting. Do you remember the look she would get when it was near feeding time?" Manny places his glass on the table and stiffens.

"Of course I do. She would eye you up as if you were her next meal. Keeping her well-paid was a chore in itself. If she wasn't so damn skilled at her job, I wouldn't have bothered." Manny takes a long drag on his cigar, blowing out circles instead of a stream of smoke.

The smell of it draws me back to the couch. I'm not much of a smoker, but when I'm here, I can hardly resist. I open the box and grab a cigar for myself. "He has the same one. I won't be able to get him out of prison if this trial doesn't move quickly. You can't put someone like that behind bars for too long. I can already see him struggling." Manny gets up, moves to his desk, pulls out a stack of thin black-bound books, and starts skimming through them. "For some reason, Cain is important to her. I just don't know the why yet." I remain stoic while adjusting myself to see him. Demanding Manny's undivided attention, making every bit of eye contact he will allow.

When Ali left, it put a kibosh on the trajectory of our plans. These two hate each other far too much for little reason. However, Manny is a man of business. He understands what we are working towards. The cost of losing control over the district isn't worth letting the possibility of Ali joining our organization again just go. If we are going to make our move to take control of the entire district, we need that additional layer of lethal power. "He is her prodigy. I saw the mark." Manny stares at me and pulls out his chair. Hearing this sort of lead I know he is locked in.

Manny plops into his chair and takes a deep breath, releasing a deep rumble from his chest that vibrates through the room. Darkness shadows around his eyes, shifting from human to reptile as small onyx scales form on his skin. His nails morph into talons, changing the pitch of the desktop echoes' rhythmic taps. These two have too much history for Manny not to get involved. "What do you need me to do?" he growls.

7

Lily

My eyes open to the morning light filtering through the curtains. Hope leaves me expecting to see Adam lying beside me in our bed. Rolling over only to find that hope is not enough. The cold vacant spot beside me speaks volumes, echoing the growing silence between us. At the same time, the chill of uncertainty replaces the longing for the warmth of his presence. We've been falling head-first to our demise for some time now. Maybe Sam answering the phone yesterday was a blessing in disguise, opening the door I need to walk out of this relationship.

From what Sam said, Adam was infuriated over him answering my phone. Since then, it has been radio silence. Adam has done this before, and honestly, I don't have the energy or willpower to go through it all again. The silent treatment, the binge drinking, maybe even sleeping around again thinking it will hurt me. I will never understand why we can't just open our relationship. If he wants to sleep with other people, I am perfectly fine with that. It would be better that way. No, it would be safer. All it takes is a conversation.

With a stretch and yawn, I throw back the covers and slowly let my aching feet touch the cool wooden floor. Clearing my head of hypotheticals and the uncertainties racing through me. I allow the anticipation of a new day to invigorate me as I shuffle to the closet. I push Adams's clothes to the side to get to the tiny section of my clothes. It may not be much, but at least I have some room in here.

It's different from the colors and textures of clothes I had collected over the years. After I moved in Adam had me donate all the outfits he didn't like me to wear. The screeching sound of hangers sliding along the rod punctuates the quiet morning, reminding me that none of this is okay. I select an outfit that mirrors my mood – a black cotton t-shirt and my favorite pair of jeans. I shouldn't have to be left to wonder in silence about him. Mr. M is probably right. Maybe Adam isn't part of my story. He has never been wrong before.

Leaving the bedroom I turn the corner towards the bathroom. I catch a glimpse of myself in the mirror, still half awake. Washing the sleep from my face, I force a subtle smile. I can make myself happy. I don't need Adam to do that for me. I've held onto this for far too long. I need to tell Adam we are over. When he decides to come back, I'm leaving him. I can't afford to change my mind.

My stomach rumbles, demanding the need for substance. With Adam not coming home, I'm going to head straight into starvation mode. If I don't feed it correctly, this thing inside me eats away at whatever it can clasp onto. It's like having the flu that never leaves you and only gets worse the longer I don't eat. It starts with widespread pain throughout my body. First, I begin to ache. Nothing too severe, more like a warning that I am reaching into dangerous territory and have gone too long.

Every muscle and joint works against me as I move. Then, the pain morphs into a deep burning sensation with every step or sway of a limb or, worse, a stabbing feeling that nearly cripples me with every wave of pain. Fatigue is a constant companion to the starvation process. Disrupting my sleep and leaving me drained. My cognitive abilities become affected as well if it goes on longer than a day, causing me to have difficulties with concentration and memory, forcing me to transform into a feral beast.

As it takes more from my body, forcing the change, all my senses work overtime, overwhelming me—the heightened sensitivity to every stimulus like light, noise, smell, temperature…touch. I think I can hold out till tomorrow. I won't be a cheater, but if I become too far gone, I will have little choice as it takes over me. I refuse to be that person. *Ding Ding.* Flipping my phone over to see the screen, I find a picture of Samael taking over my background. "Hello?"

"Mornin', sweet cheeks. How's the sea cucumber holding up?" I groan, knowing that this will either be a stellar conversation or Sam will be absolutely insufferable.

"Sweet cheeks? Really? Out of all the cliché names you could come up with, that's the one you decided on?" Samael chuckles through the line. I put the phone on speaker and grab my make-up bag.

"Well, as I was going through the list this morning, I had to nix a few. I started with beautiful, then gorgeous, pooh bear. I fought with goddess and queen for a minute there, too." Pulling out the minimal, I start working on putting my eyeliner and mascara on.

Yup, insufferable. That's what he decided on. "Why not Lily?

I do have a name." I pull the eyeliner away from my face.

"True, but what I would like to call you is *mine.*" I have to catch my breath—the idea of being his, belonging to Samael. No, I can't think this way. Not yet.

"He didn't come home last night," I say and finish up my eyeliner. I catch a quiet growl coming through the phone.

"Did he not come home last night, or did something else happen that you're uncomfortable telling me? I am a lawyer. I do have ways of finding things or…making them disappear if that is what you would prefer." I watch a small grin morph on my face as I bring the mascara brush to my eye. Why does he feel so safe to me? There's no way he can know about Adam's and my history. I've never reported Adam, gone to the police, or even made a fucking social media post about our relationship.

"Why are you calling me, Sam?" I huff, putting the mascara away and zipping up my makeup bag.

"Well, I was calling to see if you were interested in meeting me at the coffee shop so I can see you get all flustered when I pay for you again. Maybe, this time, you can enjoy a muffin instead of shoving it all into your mouth at once. Which, by the way, was quite impressive, I might add." I put the bag into the vanity drawer. I am heading there anyway. It's basically a morning ritual at this point.

Besides, who am I to say no to free tea and food when they're offered? At least this time, I won't be forced to accept the kindness of a stranger. I hate feeling like I owe people.

"Sure, I can be there in about twenty minutes." I walk downstairs, keeping the phone on speaker and shoving it behind my bra strap while gathering my things.

"Good, I'll order your usual." I pull my shirt open and look at the screen. He hung up on me. What the fuck. He doesn't even know my usual. I grab my phone, toss it into my purse, and head out the door.

Stepping outside, the crisp autumn air embraces me with the season's comfort. The rustling of dry leaves beneath my boots reminds me that summer is gone. It amazes me how fast the world changes. Closing the door behind me, I take a deep breath, inhaling the scent of the leaves and the promise of change. I want to feel some sort of way for planning to leave Adam, but I can't.

Thinking back on all the broken promises, growing lies, and the fear seeded into me is enough reason to get out while I still can. No person should have to deal with any of these feelings.

The quiet of the morning is welcoming. It's a perfect time to practice some mindfulness. With slow, concentrated breaths, I take a moment to appreciate how the light filters through the trees as I pass them—creating a kaleidoscope of colors that leaves me to wonder if the trees know how beautiful they are.

A gentle hum breaks my concentration as a familiar, sleek, blacked-out car moves closer to the curb. The gentle purr of its engine momentarily consumes my attention, drowning out the city's ambient noise. The tires meet the pavement with a soft, confident whisper, signaling its arrival. Tinted windows conceal any glimpse of the occupants. My heartbeat quickens as the front passenger-side window rolls down, revealing an air of mystery that leaves me both intrigued and apprehensive.

"Mornin' there, missy. I was sent to give you a lift." Bending down, I glimpse a cheery man with a reddish beard wearing a golf hat sitting in the driver's seat.

"I'm sorry, sir, but I think you have the wrong person. I didn't call for a ride." The man grabs the shifter and places the car in the park. The sound of the driver's door opening heightens my senses and my heartbeat begins to bound in my chest. He steps out of the vehicle and walks towards me.

I start memorizing his description just in case. White male, five foot ten, maybe eleven, red beard, brownish golf hat, medium build. "No, I am confident I do not have the wrong person. Names Hal. I'm Sammy's driver and honorary bestie." He reaches his hand towards me to shake it. "It's a pleasure to meet the lady that has ol' Sammy boy wound up tighter than a top." His accent is so unique, I wonder where it's from. An air of relief washes over me. I reach out and shake his hand.

"Lily, but how does Samael know where I am?" I really want to know. He's so presumptuous and I barely know this man. Hal lets go of my hand and opens the back door, motioning for me to get in.

"He has his ways. Ya know he's a hot shot lawyer now, ain'tcha?" He beams with pride. My phone dings in my purse. Pulling it out, I can see a text from Sam.

I've sent my driver, Hal, to get you. He should be there shortly. Don't worry, he's mostly harmless. As long as you don't get him talking, then there is no saving you.

I can feel the grin creeping up as a picture of the man standing before me comes into view on my screen.

"Ah, late again with the warnings. I keep telling that man he needs to move faster than me. He never could beat me at any race. One time, when we were kids, Sammy thought that he could beat me in a foot race. Little did he remember his best buddy, who admittedly is a bit of a cheat. I tossed my drink into the grass where he'a be runnin', and wouldn't you know he ran right into it and kissed the ground faster than you can blink!" Hal belly laughs.

With a gracious smile, I step towards the open car door. Hal smiles back at me with the biggest grin I have ever witnessed, creating small wrinkles around his eyes. I attempt to enter the back seat gracefully, but my feet have a different plan. My foot catches on absolutely nothing but air.

Stumbling forward, I desperately try to regain my balance by wobbling in all directions. Hal lunges ahead, grabs my arm, and pulls me back before I crack my head on the frame of the door. My cheeks flush with embarrassment as Hal belly laughs beside me, "Oh, you two are a match made in heaven with moves like that!" I place my hand on the car to steady myself and take my time getting into it.

I giggle, "Yeah, I'm a professional gravity tester. This spot was due for its randomized inspection." Hal begins closing the door on me.

"Well, did it pass?" His happiness is infectious, I relax into the leather seat and fasten my seatbelt.

"Oh, absolutely! With flying colors!"

8

Samael

Sipping my drink, I glance back at the door. My heartbeat quickens, caught in a rhythm of anticipation. This delicate dance between my excitement and uncertainty is one that I am unfamiliar with—a tingling energy courses through me. Maybe the coffee here is more potent than I'm used to. In my line of work, my days are filled with cases and delicate maneuvers through the judicial system that require unwavering precision and systematic planning. Although, right now, the prospect of her arrival occupies my thoughts more than Cain's case.

The aroma of freshly brewed coffee blends with my nervous excitement, creating a unique moment I haven't experienced since the first time I stepped into a courtroom. Seconds stretch on, each one filled with growing promise and hope. Allowing the shred of humanity I have left to show its face and suspend this moment, narrowing the balance between anticipative expectations and reality. I shift through the papers of Cain's case in an attempt to regain control of my restless energy. Each document is a temporary escape merely a fleeting diversion as the thoughts of Lily creep back in.

"Order for Samael," the blonde barista from yesterday calls out. Filing my papers back into my briefcase, I tuck my chair into place and retrieve our drinks. Thankfully, this is Lily's favorite spot.

At least, that's what the barista told me. She went on for at least fifteen minutes about how Lily is here nearly every day. It seems that my girl is a creature of habit. She has apparently never ordered anything other than a London Fog tea with soy milk. I slide a sizable tip into their collection jar. Everything has a price, and despite the information being freely given, it's worth a lot to me.

The chimes ring and the familiar face of Judge Michael walks in. I grab Lily's drink and keep my head down, trying to blend in with the background. One can never be sure when business will arise. Abandoning my table, I slink into a corner seat, strategically facing the entrance. My eyes dart around, staying vigilant for Lily's impending arrival while maintaining whatever anonymity I can cultivate from the shadows rising around me.

Nonetheless, I can sense Judge Michael's unshakeable and familiar energy. My hackles rise beneath the weight of the invisible shadows coating my skin, an instinctual reaction to the presence of this unexpected threat. The sound of his footsteps getting closer evokes the ire long felt. It's one thing to deal with him at work. There I can keep my composure and maintain the emotional distance the job requires, shaping the false reality of our existence beyond mortal comprehension.

Apart from that, this is my territory, and I will not allow him to pollute it with his holier-than-thou shit. Judge Michael pulls the chair out beside me, unbuttons his jacket, and sits. Squaring my shoulders, I project my aura towards him as a reminder that this is not the time or place. My shadows flit around and encapsulate us in a domain imperceptible to everyone else's primitive senses. "Cute place you got here." Michael takes a sip of his drink and avoids my eye contact.

"It is. I think I might come here more often. Have you tried the breakfast sandwiches?" I ask just a little too surly. If there is one thing that needs to be avoided, it is making a scene.

"Not yet. I'll keep that in mind the next time I stop by." Michael put his cup on the table. Shifting in my chair, I reach down to grab my briefcase. Feeling the weight, I know my tainted pistol is still inside. Deadly to mortals and immortals alike. However, when used against an immortal, they are consumed by illusions of deception and discouragement, forcing them to believe they have lost all connection to their source, driving them to embody their darkest selves.

I have only used it once in my life. Years ago, I was attacked by one of Ali's followers. She and her followers were always a force against nature; this time, she went too far. Ali recruited here and there, which isn't unusual.

She habitually purged the ones she felt were unworthy or when she had simply gotten tired of them. One of her changelings went wild before Ali was able to cull him. I thought I had killed him until he started screaming for her. That's when I learned of its true power. Now that Cain is around, there is no telling if she has more wandering around the city.

"To what do I owe the pleasure of this unexpected visit, Mikey? I can't say I've seen you around these parts recently." Hearing me call him by his nickname catches his attention. I love pissing him off.

"First off, don't call me that. Nobody calls me that anymore. Second, the reason for my visit is because we need to talk. This is your official notice. I'll be at St. Augustine's at nightfall." Michael stands from his chair. "This is a matter for the ferryman's table." Michael tucks in his chair and fastens his jacket, "I'll see you in court." he scoffs, leaving with his drink in hand.

Michael combs his hair back with his free hand, politely nodding at each person he walks past as he exits the shop. One can never be sure when dealing with Michael. Rumor has it that last week, he executed somebody from his street team. Very unlike him, with his rigid sense of morals. I've never known Michael to do anything but offer charity to those desperate for redemption. Even before he became the head of his organization, Michael would send someone else to do his dirty work. He never could handle the bloodshed required to stay at the top.

Taking a deep breath, the shadows that enveloped me scatter around the shop, grabbing onto every sin these people offer up. Every person in this building goes about their business without hesitation or reluctance. Their expressions and actions are calm and serene despite the chaotic scene unfolding around them. Existing in their abstract lives, impervious to the turmoil, spawning a surreal ignorance between their daily lives and the surrounding chaos. Like leeches, the shadows collect my breakfast directly from their souls, and one by one, I am satiated.

By consuming the essence of their respective transgressions left on display for the taking I am restored to balance. Their short and fragmented vitality dwindles further into the dark sanctuary I provide, claiming my divine right to their atrocities.

As the last shadow scours for a meal suitable for its master, the bells of the door chime, and the final shadow latches onto Lily's sins and swiftly delivers them to me. Savoring the rich blend of forbidden flavors, the irresistible morsel dances on my palate, igniting a rush of pleasure that stiffens me. Constricting the space in my slacks, the building pressure demands its release and leaving an unforgettable imprint on my senses.

As Lily walks closer to me, my arousal only grows. The need within me begs for its priestess to come and collect it. Fiery blue tendrils caress her hourglass form, echoing an insatiable hunger that seeks resolve. Standing from my seat, the whispering muse before me compels my true self to abandon all hope and give myself to her tantalizing promises.

Wild and untamed desire roars with the intensity of a thousand storms in my chest. This fiery passion fuels the hearth of my ambitions, pushing me to reach for my temptress, leaving me vulnerable to the sting of unfulfilled longing. I hardly realize I'm weaving through tables, chairs, and people until I finally get to her.

With Lily in my grasp, I find solace in the gentleness that resides within her. Her beautiful brown eyes lock onto mine, showing me her pain. Falling into a trance, I watch as images of her love, hunger, yearning, wishes, delights, and fears put themselves on full display. My heart wrenches for her.

I lean in and our lips meet, an explosion of sensations heightened by the collision of desire, sending shivers down my spine. Lily's breath is warm against my skin, mingling with my heat in a dance of shared, unexpected longing. Kissing with tender exploration is a slow and deliberate meeting of lips that conveys a hunger, a yearning, building in the silent spaces between us.

Our mouths move in perfect synchrony, with a choreography of passion that speaks volumes without a single word. The dance of our tongues, wrapped in an intimate tango that explores the depths of our unholy connection. Every brush of Lily's lips, every subtle nibble, sends ripples of pleasure through my entire being, igniting a fire that burns with an intensity I have never dreamed of.

Time stands still as we lose ourselves in the intoxicating exchange. Fingers tangled in hair, bodies pressed together in a fervent embrace. The world outside ceases to exist, and in that moment, there is only the sensation of being consumed by her flames.

As the kiss deepens, this crescendo of longing and passion crashes over me like waves. Lily's radiant flames speaking a language of their own, communicating a love that surpasses the limitations of words. From now on, no matter the cost, she is mine, and I'm hers—my dark goddess of destruction.

9

Lily

Walking into the coffee shop, I felt my energy waning with each step, like a dim flame flickering in the cold grasp of my hunger. My stomach is protesting with every desperate contraction. Its hollow ache, a relentless reminder of the absence of a suitable meal. The pangs, rhythmic, like a cruel melody playing in the background of my consciousness. I never expected that he would offer himself to me this way.

Desire courses through my veins like an electric current that sets my senses ablaze. It's not a gentle whisper but a commanding presence, an urgent call that refuses to be ignored. The mere proximity to Samael is enough to make me salivate with anticipation. My thoughts are consumed by the allure of what could be as the boundaries of fidelity blur within the intoxication of his kiss.

The feeling of longing is bittersweet, a delicate balance between the thrill of pursuit and the ache of unfulfilled yearning. As my hunger dwindles, the sensations of my body become more profound – the rapid heartbeat, my desperate shallow breaths, and a flush of warmth that spreads through my core. Every touch, no matter how fleeting, draws Samael's lust from his lips like ripe fruit for the taking.

With each passing moment, I savor the delicate balance between hunger and fulfillment. The ritual of consuming his need morphs into a celebration, like a sacrilegious communion, as he offers up nourishing elements that sustain my life. In the aftermath of satiating hunger, I find myself restored and reborn. No longer am I held captive by the depraved emptiness that haunts my every step.

As our lips slowly part, a shared breath lingers between us. I swallow hard, savoring his tart essence, which remains on my lips, etching this moment into my memory. Silently praying that it will forever be imprinted on my soul. The world slowly comes crashing back towards me as I gaze into his eyes. "Hey there." I exhale shakily, steadying my breath.

Samael's gentle touch interrupts my focus as his fingers delicately weave through the strands of hair that have fallen across my face. The sensation is subtle, like a whispered caress, as his fingers lightly gather the stray strands and sweep them away, tucking them deftly behind my ear. His touch radiates heat and reassurance, a tactile connection that momentarily pulls me out of whatever occupied my thoughts. I move my head towards his hand, trying to fall into the gentle and relaxing hold he offers.

Samael brushes his open palm across my cheek and holds the weight of my head. Seizing the opportunity, I close my eyes for a fleeting second, settling into his grasp, acknowledging the simple yet intimate gesture as peace envelops my body. Slowly drawing my eyes open again, I meet Sam's lascivious stare. There's a transient connection, this shared moment of understanding communicated through an unspoken language of physical closeness that only we can understand. The strands of hair, once a subtle barrier, now lifted, revealing a clearer view of the world and an unobstructed fiery Samael.

As Samael's fingers withdraw, I'm grateful for the brief interruption. It's a small act that carries a touch of concern and consideration. The brush of his hand dwells on my cheek like a silent prayer for it to return. My skin begs for his comfort, sinfully discovered. "If I was a better man I would say that I'm sorry, but I refuse to apologize for giving you anything you need and more than you deserve." His voice resonates in a deep timbre that carries an unavoidable gravity with each uttered word.

Clearing my throat, I take a step back to fix my outfit. A flush of warmth spreads across my face, and a prickling feeling creeps up my neck. The sudden awareness of everyone's sight on us intensifies, and my heart quickens in sync with the rising tide of embarrassment. It's as if an invisible spotlight has focused solely on me. "Can I have that coffee now?" I brush my hand down and off his chest.

Sam's eyes widen. "I thought I got you your usual. Do you usually get coffee?" I giggle at his panic, watching him run back to the table and grab both to-go cups. With long strides, he reaches me within seconds. "Here, you can take mine. It's black coffee unless you want me to order something else." Sam's cheeks start to flush, and I snatch the cup he holds closer.

"I'm just fucking with you. Although, if this tea is messed up, we might have to discuss precisely what I need there, handsome." As I bring the cup to my lips, the first sip sends a wave of pleasure through me.

The warmth of the tea spreads from my chest, radiating outwards, and I feel an almost meditative calm settle over me. It's a sensation beyond the physical – a balm for the soul. With each sip, I appreciate the craftsmanship that went into brewing this perfect cup. Giving Sam a side-eyed glance as I murmur, "You're lucky." I lick my lips and playfully smile.

Samael practically skips back to the table once more, abandoning me for a moment. He grabs a briefcase, walks behind me, and opens the door. "How about we go somewhere else?" He steps behind the door, holding it open for me. As I get outside, I'm greeted by the crisp air of the fall morning. Samael abandons the door and walks over to the car Hal is driving and leaves his briefcase in it. "So where are we off to, my Goddess?" His voice is low and tempting. The sun casts a warm glow, and a gentle breeze rustles the leaves overhead.

"I'm actually on my way to the bookshop after this. We can go through the park if you're not too busy." I suggest, my voice deceptively confident. Sam wraps his arm around mine, linking us together.

"I'm never too busy for you." He lifts my head gently by the chin and tenderly kisses my forehead, warming me more than the tea ever could.

With each step, the concrete beneath my feet gives way to the softer texture of a well-trodden path leading to the nearby park. The familiar route unfolds before me, a mosaic of sights and sounds that mark the transition from the bustling urban landscape to the serene embrace of nature. "Samael," I say, my lips savoring every syllable before pausing to gather my thoughts. "Why did you kiss me?" His face shifts in a way that shows he's just as much at a loss for words as I am over this morning's events.

"I told you that I'm not going to apologize, and please call me Sam. Samael is far too formal." Sam runs his fingers through his hair as we come to a halt. "You wear your suffering on your sleeve whether you know it or not, Goddess. While you are in my presence, I refuse to let it consume you." His words feel like pouring salt on a fresh wound. How could he possibly know what my suffering looks like? I've been living day in and day out, starving for more than he could imagine.

I crave a home that doesn't feel like a war zone every time I enter it. I am yearning for friends and family who are either dead or have disappeared because I was forced to push them away. I am hungry for something or someone to make me feel safe, only to find it when I'm in the most danger I have ever been in.

Where is my safety? My sense of security? My sense of belonging? The sting of my fingernails digging into my palms is the only thing I have to prevent me from completely losing my shit. Sam grabs onto the back of my arms and pulls me closer to him.

Sam leans forward, jaw set and eyes blazing with a fury that mirrors my own. "When you are finally mine and only mine, it will never happen again." Sam says with confidence as he goes to touch my cheek. I pull my head back.

Sam drops his hand and I rip my arm out of his gentle hold "You have no idea what you're talking about. You don't even know the first thing about me." I walk away, hoping my emotions don't betray me as my eyes burn, threatening to release a cascade of tears.

The rhythmic tap of our footsteps starts again. Sam yells behind me, "You don't think I know you?!" His footsteps grow louder until they are right behind me. "I know more about you than you think." As we approach the park, a subtle shift in atmosphere occurs. It's taking all my control to not strangle him. Sam's face contorts into the vision of shock as I poke my finger into his chest.

"Okay then, tell me hot shot. What the fuck do you think you know about me?" I roar. Sam stands taller, squaring his shoulders and fixes his suit jacket. His eyes soften while the air around us grows warmer than it was a moment ago.

"I know you always order the same thing at that coffee shop. I know you always tip your barista the same amount as your bill. I know that when you get nervous, you blush and smile with your eyes rather than your mouth when you're happy. I know that you have been through hell and back, fighting the same thing that has given you your freedom." Sam walks closer to me.

"I know you are scared to leave Adam, and that's the only reason you stay with him. I may have only known you for a little over a day, but I sure as fuck know that you felt the same thing that I did the moment we locked eyes. It was as if the universe was pulling us towards each other, defying all rationality. And I know that you are the most stubborn, goofy woman I have ever met, and I will do everything in my power to move the heavens and earth for you." Sam gets into my space and leans in, lowering his voice to a near whisper.

"Not because it's in my nature to care for those I hold dear to me, but because you deserve all the kindness and love the world has denied you." My breath catches in my throat, and I struggle to find words or make sense of the overwhelming wave of emotions crashing over me. There's a numbness, a disconnect between mind and body, and it's as if I've been thrust into an alternate dimension where nothing makes sense.

The distant hum of city life gives way to the melodic symphony of chirping birds and rustling leaves. "Well, you're wrong about one thing. I am leaving Adam. I'm going to tell him tonight."

10

Samael

My heart races like a relentless drumbeat echoing in my chest. The air feels charged between us, and every nerve in my body tingles with an electrified intensity. Time seems to pause for a moment, stretching into an agonizing crawl as I stare at her courage shining through. "When are you telling him?" I try to hide the range of emotions that rushes through me and fixate on the beautiful woman before me. Out of all the things I could have missed, how did I miss her strength?

"Tonight. I'll be out by the morning. I don't want to take the chance of sticking around too long and him getting any more upset than he already is. It's for the best, honestly." Lily looks down and sways slightly. While I know that I should feel more unease with how Lily speaks about Adam, I let hope take over me.

As children play around us with unrestrained joy and the distant laughter of friends engaging in conversation creates a harmonious backdrop, I can't stop some concern from bubbling up about how Lily leaving Adam will play out.

We stroll along the winding paths, and I inhale the earthy fragrance of nature and feel the dappling sunlight that filters through the canopy of trees.

The park offers a peaceful sanctuary from the unease settling in my chest. I find a quiet bench and settle in, taking a moment to absorb the serenity that envelops me. Lily sits beside me, sipping her tea in silence as if she understands that I recognize her situation is more than she has been willing to tell me.

The rustling leaves and distant chatter become a soothing soundtrack, and I immerse myself in the simple pleasure of being present in this oasis of calm before the storm begins. Lily stares at her cup as if the answers to her problems are written on the lid. "Let me come with you." I offer suddenly. "If anything, I can help you move the things you need out of the house." I can only imagine the intrepidity it takes for Lily, let alone any woman, to leave situations like hers.

Lily lifts her gaze from the ground, brushing fallen strands of her bright chestnut hair behind her ear. Her eyes betray the vulnerability that her stoic expression tries to conceal. Lily crosses her legs as she squares her shoulders, attempting to project an image of a shield that envelops her soul. Yet, the subtle quiver of her jaw and the fleeting hesitance in willingness to even look at me prove that Lily's stubbornness will win again. "I appreciate the offer, but I can handle it by myself. I have to do this on my own, for me," she says firmly.

I can sense the quiet plea in how she holds herself, like a silent call for understanding amidst this charade. The independence she projects feels like fragile armor, worn and prepared to crack under the weight of her unspoken burdens. It's a performance, a brave act to cloak herself from the world.

Yet, in her eyes, I see the powerlessness that resonates with the authenticity of her struggle. The only thing I can do is support her. "Fine, I'll keep my distance under one condition," I grumble. Lily squeezes her eyebrows together and starts to chew on her bottom lip. "I'm going to call you tonight, and you have to answer the phone, so I know you are okay." If she needs to do this on her own, then that is precisely what she will get.

As we exit the park, the autumn breeze carries a chill that touches more than just the air. Beside me, this goddess who holds my heart and soul walks silently. Her steps are lively yet somber. The rustle of fallen leaves provides a morbid accompaniment to our path as they are crushed beneath our feet.

As we get closer to the nearby bookshop, she asks me to walk with her, and concern for her well-being creeps back into my thoughts. She may think that she is putting on a good act, but the distant expression in Lily's eyes gives her away. I can hear how her laugh holds a hint of restraint.

I could show up tonight anyway, but that will only prove to her that I'm just as untrustworthy as Adam is. The crunch of the fallen leaves echoes a heaviness, as the once vibrant colors of autumn seem muted in comparison to the agonizing torment of uncertainty. Approaching the quaint bookshop, the familiarity raises her spirits in a way that makes a child gleeful in the presence of their mother. "Do you want to come in? This is my favorite place, after all," Lily practically sings.

As she opens the door, sounds both unearthly and discordant break through. A demonic choir of ominous tones, each note resonating with an eerie malevolence. A cacophony of guttural growls and dissonant harmonies emanate from within.

The air hangs heavy with an unsettling stillness as the

haunting chorus grows louder. Like a siren song, I can feel its pull drawing me in. "Well?" Lily's voice snaps me out of the trance. There doesn't seem to be a source of the music. *Bing. Bing. Bing.* The alarm on my phone blares, signaling that I have to be at the courthouse. I pull it out of my pocket and silence it.

"No, not today, my Goddess. I will soon, though." Pressing my lips to her forehead, I silently pray for her safety. "I'm sorry, I have to be at the courthouse. Don't forget to answer when I call you tonight." The familiar hum of an approaching car gradually becomes more pronounced, alerting me that Hal is here. He's getting better at his stakeouts. I hardly noticed him following us in the first place.

Before committing to leaving her, I watch Lily enter the bookshop. Slamming the car door shut feels like a nail has been put in her coffin. "I need you to call Levi and track her phone. Tell him to hack in and listen to what happens once she gets home." I fidget in my seat.

Hal watches me from the rearview mirror. "Is she alright? What happened?" he asks, concern dripping into his voice.

* * *

As I approach the witness stand, I feel the courtroom's attention shift toward me: Judge Michael's stern expression, the jury's watchful eyes, and the energy of the courtroom intensifying with each witness I interview on the stand. Methodically, I engage in only brief exchanges with each witness to establish a swift rapport and tactfully guide them toward the narrative I paint so that there is no room for doubt on Cain's feigned innocence.

With a series of calculated questions, I elicit a clear and compelling account of the murder from the kid who recorded it—navigating through the details, probing him with each inconsistency and every weakness I found.

It isn't fair that I'm so hard on the kid, but if he wants to stick his nose in places where they don't belong, I will make sure this is an experience he will never forget. If he's lucky, Michael will recruit him after this. He is everything that Michael strives for when building his team. Young, honest, easily swayed to righteousness, and oblivious to how the world works.

This room is a stage that I control. The stakes are high, and every question I pose is a move in the chess game of legal persuasion. The jury's reactions and the subtle shifts in the atmosphere are my indicators, guiding my approach as I navigate the balance of challenging the witness while maintaining professional decorum.

While the promise of a hefty paycheck hangs in the balance for the jury for me to win, I want to make sure they feel as if they are making the right decision. Money can do many things, but when it's obtained in a way that makes you think you were doing it for the right reason, it comes with the added security of silence.

"Next witness, Cain Jubilee." My head shoots up at the abrupt sound of the metal chair scraping across the tile floor. Cain gets up from his seat and walks to the witness stand. A surge of fury courses through me. I can feel my jaw clench as I hastily review my notes, realizing that circumstances have forced my hand. The courtroom's attention shifts as the clicking and flashing of the media's cameras go wild. This was not part of the plan at all. I stand demanding Michael's attention in the chaos.

"Your Honor, a moment of your time, please." Michael's brows furrow and his lips grow into a thin line. With the clack of his gavel, we are dismissed for a short recess.

The door slams shut behind me as I charge into Michael's chambers. "What the fuck is that? They completely blindsided me! We had an agreement that he would not testify!" I shout. I grab the back of the chair that separates me from Michael as he tosses a file onto his desk.

"That's not how this is going to work. I don't care who you are. You will not come into my chambers and disrespect me or the process." Michael's knuckles whiten as he points at me, accentuating nearly every word. My shadows fly around the room towards me, engulfing half of the chambers into darkness as Michael becomes a beacon of light illuminating everything around him.

The battlefield between us intensifies, his light attempting to conquer my darkness. "I haven't even started disrespecting you. We made a deal, and you went back on your word once again. You want me to trust you, well then start being trustworthy." The interplay creates a warzone, where the boundaries between realms blur and redefine themselves with each adjustment.

Michael throws his head back in a fit of arrogant laughter. "When have you ever been a man of your word, Samael? How you forget just how far you have fallen. I will put you in your place every chance I get. I can see why you're drawn to him, and I will not let you get away with claiming another soul for your damned army." In a flash, metal armor with a large golden cross on the breastplate appears over Michael's robe. His battle regalia is one that I will never forget.

The room is a canvas for our battlefield, where our powers

meet, the two blending, redefining what is right and just. I'm left with no other choice.

I have to play my cards. Being at each other's throats isn't going to get me closer to her for Manny. I owe this to Manny. His friendship means too much to me. "You fucking moron, Cain has the mark!" The light radiating from Michael recedes instantaneously and his armor disappears completely. "You know just as well as I do what that means. I have seen my fair share of what that woman is capable of. So you can either cooperate or buy a tombstone." I let my powers grow, encroaching on the space Michael stands.

11

Lily

I'm so grateful for this place. There's something magical about this bookshop and Mr. M that can get me out of my head. Mr. M will never ask me for help, but I am more than happy to do it anyway. Between cleaning, organizing, and taking care of the customers, Mr. M finally has the opportunity to sit and rest. At the same time, I enjoy the simplicity of the mundane. Every so often, I catch him watching me while I work. His smile feels like a beacon of hope.

While things are slow, I try to find that book, the one I saw many years ago. I can sense it within these walls calling to me. Their melodic hymns beckon for me to read it. If only I could understand what they are saying. Do the words sound like an old Spanish or Italian dialect? Maybe both, for all I know. This is the worst game of hot and cold I have ever played. As soon as I think I am close to the book, the music changes, flitting about the room projecting from a different location.

I need to know why it chose me. Living a life deprived

of satisfaction, forever on the hunt for my next meal, isn't necessarily the kind of life that I would have chosen for myself. I sound like I'm crazy. What sort of sane person thinks a book would actually come alive and choose a person?

Nope, that's not anywhere close to sane. A more logical explanation is that I'm hallucinating or something and have finally completely lost it. At the very least, I could be having a mental breakdown. That is a distinct possibility considering that I am under a lot of stress and the sheer fact that I have been hungry for so long.

Maybe I can have a nutritional deficiency from lack of sex. I have to stop playing these games with myself. If it's not alive, then there would be no reason for me to go from a normal, average, everyday person to this.

"Penny for your thoughts?" As Mr. M takes his glasses off his nose, he holds out a tiny brass-colored coin with a soft smile.

"For you, there's no charge," I say softly. He slips the coin into his pocket as his eyes dart back and forth as if analyzing my face. "You've done so much for me over the years that I hate to ask you for your help." Mr. M places his hand on the small of my back and guides me to our chairs. "I've decided that I'm going to leave Adam. I'm telling him tonight. I'm going to need somewhere to stay until I can get onto my feet. I wouldn't ask-"

"Don't you even dare finish that sentence. You are like a daughter to me. You are more than welcome to stay here for however long you need to. Never question if you are welcome in my home. I still have your room upstairs all set up, just as you left it." His stern demeanor startles me. The closer he gets to me, the easier it is to see the bags under his eyes.

Mr. M's voice cracks, "I'm just so thankful you realize your situation isn't ideal before you come upon any considerable danger." Mr. M rushes forward, embracing me in the tightest hug I think he ever has. "I am so proud of you, Lily." He pulls away just slightly and locks eyes with me. "I love you to the moon and back. It's unfortunate that you're an adult, my dear, I would adopt you on the spot."

I didn't even notice I was crying until he wipes the tears from my cheeks. "Thank you." I try to mutter the words out clearly, but the emotion that has its hold on me is dragging years of repressed emotions to a head. Curling up in his arms, I let it all out. The fear, the hate, the feeling of being strong all the time falls out of me. All this time, blinded by my pride in being independent, I can finally relax.

As I calm down, Mr. M sits me in my chair and gets me a box of tissues and a cup of tea. The fire comforts me as I'm given a crocheted blanket to curl up with. The heart of the fire puts me into a hypnotic trance, I find a sense of tranquility and peace settle over me.

So many times today, the walls I have built to protect me crumble. This must be what it is like to have things fall into place. With each crackle and pop of the firewood, I settle more into the solace that Mr. M and his shop offer. "Can I get you a book, dear? A story just might help you calm your nerves." There is no masking the concern laced in his voice.

"Actually, there has been a book that I have been looking for, but I can't find it anywhere. I saw it many years ago and recently remembered it. It was written in another language, and I think it was bound in leather or something close to it." I nervously explain. Mr. M draws his lips into a straight line and rubs the back of his neck.

"The oldest books I have are dated back to around 15 A.D. However, I'm unsure how you would have seen them. I keep them locked in a specially designed vault to preserve them. I would consider allowing it if they weren't so delicate, but I'm sorry I can't. They are just too precious." Mr. M lowers his head with a subtle sigh.

I feel a tightness in my chest. A physical manifestation of a letdown. It's as if the air has thickened, making it harder to breathe. The reality of how this played out doesn't align with the picture I painted in my head.

At least, I know that I am not completely insane. There is a book in this shop that resembles my memory; it's just unobtainable. "Although, I do believe I have something similar that I can bring out for you." Mr. M's voice breaks through my introspection.

In an instant, Mr. M disappears to the back of the shop. Something similar? What could conceivably be identical to a book that has its own ominous choir? The shuffle of Mr. M's footsteps draws closer at a pace that resembles skipping. "I found it!" His eyes beam with anxious anticipation and a wanderlust of excitement to share this treasure.

As he places the book on the table, I understand his enthusiasm completely. This might be the second oldest book I have seen in my entire life. The thought of touching feels forbidden; however, the willpower to listen to that feeling is long gone.

"This, my dear, is from a century or two later than the books I keep in my vault. I'm particularly proud of this one. Some people believe it is a precursor to the Malleus Maleficarum, however I refuse to subscribe to these notions. I believe this is written by a completely separate author and was a collection of creatures that inspired the stories of the Grimm Brothers, but that's just my fun little thought. It has been passed down in my family for generations and-" Mr. M clears his throat, dragging his chair closer to mine. "I would like to share it with you." My eyes well up again. This old man who has rescued me from the world, saved me from myself, and has been a devoted father figure I love so dearly wants to share his family heirlooms with me.

"I would love to read it with you, M." I reply fervently, my fingers reaching out for this precious heirloom. The cover, weathered by time, feels delicate beneath my fingertips. As I open the pages, the musty scent of history wafts into the air, transporting me to a world long gone. Even to my untrained eye, I can see that each word was meticulously penned by the hands of some ancient scribe or priest. The paper is nearly tan, resembling more of what I imagine parchment to look like. As I turn the pages, they crinkle with a gentle protest, revealing inked illustrations and intricate golden borders that frame the text.

My skin buzzes with increasing intensity as I turn each page, discovering a world of old, transforming into a world of gruesome fantasy. Carefully painted pictures beyond anything I could imagine paired with titles of supernatural creatures that have fueled stories and nightmares for a millennia.

Vampire, dragon, doppelganger, aboleth, basilisk, lich, gorgon, chimera, a seemingly never-ending collection of monsters. Each creature has an entire page dedicated to the artistic creativity of the author and the careful brush strokes of its painter.

The vampire chapter pulls me in with its depiction of a creature crouching over its prey, blood spilling from its lips with fangs bared, and its long, spindly fingers reaching out in front of it. The ashen dragon of the next chapter is wrapped around golden coins that shimmer in the firelight.

Taking in the craftsmanship of each page, nearing the end, I read "Succubus." I gently slide my fingers across the image as a strange familiarity with the woman on the page creeps into me, with long, beautiful hair and eyes that beg you to lose yourself in them. Her artistically crafted curves resemble *Titan's Bacchanal of the Andrians*, a personification of lust incarnate. "She's beautiful. Is this what they really thought they looked like?"

"Oh yes, there are few artistic works around that depict succubi as ugly, horrendous creatures. However, they are always said to present as a beautiful woman." Stillness and curiosity settle into the room.

My mind is not willing to consider looking away from her. Mr. M's voice changes to a deeper ominous tone. I like to call it his storybook voice, and I'm lost to them both. "According to these texts, the origin of the first succubus is unknown. It reads that they are a grotesque creature with deformed horns, elongated fingers, and claws. They attack lustful men at night, preferring those who are religiously minded more than any other." Mr. M's fumbles around his words as if trying to protect my non-existent modesty.

"According to the text, the succubus seek out these men in their sleep and drain them of their life force. They don't normally kill their prey and will return to the same victim multiple times in their dreams to feast." I swallow hard, realizing why she is so familiar to me as Mr. M goes on.

An immediate heaviness builds in the pit of my stomach. It was as if I had swallowed an invisible weight, which had settled there, pulling everything within me down. The more Mr. M tells me about the succubus, the more my discomfort grows. This isn't a book of fairy tale monsters. This is a monster hunter's manual, and I'm one of them.

12

Samael

With how today has gone, I can't expect this meeting to go any better than what happened in Michael's office. Michael became particularly uneasy after I told him about Cain and the mark. He was able to call a recess until tomorrow. At least now we have time to figure out how to stop Cain from going on the stand. Hal pulls up to the bar where we are meeting. If there is one place where everyone agrees to be neutral territory, it's this dump. More shady deals have happened here than even I know of.

The air inside St. Augustine's is thick with a mix of stale smoke, cheap booze, and the faint scent of piss. The dim, flickering fluorescent lights barely illuminate the worn-out stools that are like the chipped counter. The bartender, August, still bears his weary eyes, which proves he's seen too much in this world. Wiping down a glass with a rag that has clearly seen better days, we nod to each other, silently acknowledging our presence.

August hasn't changed in all the years I have been coming

to this bar. Between his puffy face and sizable round belly, it's easy to see that he found his way to the bottom of a bottle. When he isn't behind the bar, August is seen sitting at a barstool in the corner, smoking a cigarette.

The usuals stay huddled in the shadows as their faces become obscured by the haze of cigarette smoke. This has to be one of the last bars that still has a jukebox. Despite the dull hum it emits, it still plays the same old tune from an era nearly forgotten. The cracked linoleum floor beneath my feet sticks slightly as I walk through the narrow walkway of mismatched tables and rickety chair.

Once decorated with faded posters and peeling paint, the walls are now bare and scarred with the marks of time. A dartboard hangs crookedly on the far wall, while the lone uneven pool table in the center attracts a small crowd. Their rowdy laughter blends with the distant sounds of traffic outside.

St. Augustine's atmosphere is a peculiar mix of nostalgia and decay, as if in a perpetual limbo. Conversations here are always spoken in hushed tones. It creates a dull murmur that is made complete with the occasional clinking of glasses. Us regulars and longtime parishioners have always found solace in this bar's anonymity. The old timers used to call it church, and not a single one of them missed church on Sunday.

I take a seat on a wobbly stool at the bar. Thankfully, I remembered to change out of my suit before I showed up. The cracked vinyl of my bar stool sticks to my jeans pocket. I can feel it curling under my ass cheek as I attempt to make myself comfortable.

August knows me well enough to make me the usual. A cocktail that contains orange liqueurs, lime, brandy, vodka, and some sweet and sour. A warm sense of comfort fills me as I sip the tart drink. I remember the first time I came to church with my father.

Dad had me sit behind the bar with August. He said it was important for me to learn the family business from an outsider's perspective. So, I took over bartending for the evening, giving August the night off while I followed Dad's instructions to note everything happening around me. At the night's end, he had me tell him what I saw and heard. It was his way of teaching me how to pay attention to my surroundings amid chaos.

That was our routine for many Sundays. I would bartend, and Dad would do business. He would always tell me, drinking one of these, *"If ya learn anythin' from me, learn this. When you're out on business, drink somethin' light. When you're out wi'ch ya boys, drink somethin' light. You never know who's gonna be the asshole and if ya gonna have to get outta a bad sit'chation fast. Best to do it buzzed then fallin' o'er ya selves."*

Out of the corner of my eye, I catch Michael walking in. He tugs on his blue tie, loosening it from its chokehold and pulls out the stool to my right and sits down. It wouldn't kill him to dress down every once in a while. This isn't somewhere I would visit in a suit. Let alone a charcoal one at that. Without a word, August pulls an array of bottles from behind the bar, mixes them into a single glass, and drops the glass in front of Michael with a napkin. Birds of a feather, you can call us in that department. Some things never change.

"Rough day, wouldn't you agree?" Michael downs his first drink quickly, pushing the empty glass forward to let August know he wants a refill. I guess he didn't get the same lessons as I did growing up.

"I wouldn't say it's the worst," I say flatly. I'm willing to put up with only so much small talk. This isn't a get-together. This is a meeting. He asked me to come here for a reason. "So what's the weather like?" Whenever there is a meeting at the bar, it's best to talk in code. By using this code, what I'm really asking is what kind of meeting is this. If Michael says the weather is fair, that means it's an informative meeting. If he says that it looks like there is rain in the forecast, this meeting will be about resolving discourse between our districts.

Michael stands up with his refreshed glass and walks to the reserved table. Well then, I guess we are going to completely forgo the protocols then. I grab my drink and follow him up. The table is not actually reserved, but everyone is aware of what this table is for and refuses to sit at it. They call it The Ferryman's Table. The ones who know call it that, because men and women who sit here work directly for death.

Michael rubs the palm of his hand across his face as I take my seat across from him. He leaves me my preferred spot by the wall. From here, I can see the entire length of the bar and the front door. I like to see who I am in company with, even if they aren't with me or sitting at my table.

"I went to see Cain after I dismissed the court. You're right, Samael. I saw the mark. He was more than willing to show it to me. He's just like her in almost every way. However, he doesn't really seem like Ali's type," he says clearly distressed. Michael runs his hand through his honey colored hair.

I take a long pull of my drink, swallowing it in one gulp. "So now that you have your proof, what are we going to do about the case? If this goes on any longer, then there will be more deaths in that prison than either of us can cover up." Since Cain has been locked up, there have been seven dead inmates found with unexplainable blood loss. The numbers are racking up too quickly. Michael takes a sip of his drink instead of drinking the entirety of the glass in one go.

"It's not going to be a problem. I got a call from my contact at the station today. Apparently, a former employee of the Dragon's Den came in and confessed to the murder," He says skeptically as he raises an eyebrow. I want to react to this news with every fiber of my body, but I can't.

When Manny told me he would take care of it, I knew he would. He has too much invested in this to let his only lead go. I sip on my drink a bit more to keep my mouth shut. "Cain is to be released in about a week. That's as long as I can drag my feet on the paperwork and have the case dismissed. The legitimacy of this confession is bringing up questions. However, this man was able to describe in detail how he removed all the blood from that young woman's body without a single puncture wound to be found." Michael shakes as if a chill is running through him.

I don't even want to try to imagine the story Manny came up with. "So, what are we here for then?" I ask. Michael's brows draw together, creating deep lines between them. "There isn't much more we can do here, Mikey. When Cain gets out, he's going to disappear. That's what she would do, and I don't see any reason as to why he would do anything different." Michael knocks on the table, clenching his jaw.

"We need to find out why he is here in the first place. Cain isn't so young that he can't control himself. I think she sent him here. There is no other evidence that there is more than one of them in town. Not getting to the bottom of his sudden appearance is an unnecessary risk." he insists, stabbing the table's surface with one imperious finger. I stiffen with realization—the son of a bitch has a point. I've been so distracted with all the moving parts of the case and Lily that I didn't stop to think about why he showed up in the first place.

Michael is right. Cain is different from Ali's usual recruits. Cain has a record. He can be found in the system. He has a birthdate, social security number, and everything else you can think of that would make it possible for a person to be found. His creator, however, is a ghost to modern society. You either know who she is or you don't, and only a few people actually know her. With Cain popping up and pulling this stunt, it has to be a distraction.

"I'll reach out to my team and see what they can dig up. You might be onto something here, and if we can get ahead of her for once, it should work in our favor." I polish off the last of my drink and pull out my phone. It's almost time for me to call Lily.

"Well, I think this has been a successful reunion. I'll let you know if I learn anything. I expect the same." I demand. Michael finishes his drink and nods to me in agreement. We both stand up and lean the top of our chairs in unison onto the table, indicating to the regulars and August that there will be no souls ushered across the River Styx tonight. The Ferryman's table is closed...for now.

13

Lily

I let out a sigh of relief as I walk into the house. All I want is a hot shower and to curl up in bed. I should wait until tomorrow to pack my things up. As usual, I hang my coat in the closet and leave my purse on the door. The sooner I get into a hot bath, the better. The house is quiet, which means Adam still isn't home. Tossing my boots on the floor, I rush to the bathroom like my life depends on it.

The single faucet lever squeaks as I turn it to the far left so the water can be as hot as possible. I learned long ago that setting my water heater to 120 degrees Fahrenheit is the perfect temperature – hot enough to feel the sting of near-boiling water without causing any severe damage. Years of sitting in scalding hot showers forced my skin to toughen up.

Adam tried to take showers with me at the beginning of our relationship, but he couldn't handle it. I got used to ensuring I took my showers before he got home so he didn't jump in with me. Too much yelling and arguing. He called me a masochist so many times, saying that I was trying to cause red marks to get him in trouble. The mental gymnastics he had to take to jump to that conclusion must have been exhausting.

The Epsom salts call to my achy body as I toss in a few scoops, making the lavender scent blossom through the entire bathroom. The moment I peel off my bra, freedom takes hold, and a weight is lifted from my shoulders. The sting of the hot water soothes my weary muscles. My skin immediately reddens as I submerge myself in the warmth of the salty bath.

Radiating heat assaults my face as I slowly begin to relax into it. When I close my eyes, my brain starts working over time. How could I have allowed our relationship to get this far? I'm going to break his heart, but the way Adam treats me. If I could have only loved him harder. Helped him more. Done better in general. No, I can't think like that.

No matter what he has said, this isn't my fault. None of this is my fault. I take my time processing each emotion, but eventually, I shove the feelings back into myself and swallow them whole. It's time to call in the big guns.

Within seconds I find my beloved battery-operated boytoy in the second drawer in the bathroom. My B.O.B. always comes in clutch in my time of need. Purple, curved, and with a clit suction, just how I like it. After a three-second hold, B.O.B. comes to life in my hand, making promises I know he can keep. As it dips into the tub with me, the vibration sounds quiet.

Despite laying in a bathtub, I can feel myself becoming wet with anticipation. Gently stroking my inner folds, I open them up and slip B.O.B. inside. The sensation of it entering me as my inner walls conform to the shape of its shaft drives my desire to a place of no return.

The vibrations inside force me to clench down on it, and my

clit pleads for attention. I start rocking my hips back and forth in a rhythmic motion while slowly pulsing the soft, bulbous tip in and out of me. A meek groan escapes from my throat as images of Sam come to the front of my imagination.

I envision myself leaning into him this morning, feeling the intensity of his desires consuming us both. The longing to taste him again overwhelms me. At the same time, the memory of tobacco and sin permeates the air, overpowering the lavender entirely. I picture his hands grabbing a hold of my ass while I ride his face, pushing the boundaries of my desire and leaving him covered, drowning in a pool of my sweet nectar as I tug on my hardened nipples.

With another click, the suction starts, giving my clit the attention it screams out for, sending me to a plane beyond this reality, as the painful need of release bubbles to its crux. Images of Sam driving himself into me as he grips my throat, adding just the right amount of pressure, giving me the most beautiful necklace. I refuse to let my panting distract me as my orgasm nearly has me unfolding, crumbling to the idea of us in the thralls of cardinal sin. "What the fuck are you doing?"

The gruff sound of Adam's voice turns the water ice cold. "I'm obviously trying to get off since you've been missing. Speaking of that, what have you been doing, Adam?" I bite back. Every promise B.O.B. made was destroyed by Adam's icy tone.

There's no time for disappointment. Adam's brows draw together and his jaw begins to tense. Challenging him may not be the most brilliant idea, but I won't back down this time. Enough is enough. I'm leaving whether he likes it or not. I hold down the button and shut off B.O.B. while simultaneously pulling it out of me, and hope this turns Adam on instead from the pressure building in my chest.

"Standing here wondering why my fucking bitch prefers a piece of plastic over me. Am I not enough for you, Lily? Do I not satisfy your every need? Your every desire? Tell me, Lil, what *am* I supposed to feel walking in on my cheating whore of a girlfriend fuck herself in a goddamned bathtub?!"

The scent of his anger takes over the room with an oppressive hold. Everything in me says to curl my tail under my ass and bow to his every whim. It would be safer. The last time he was like this, I was in the hospital for three days. Adam is taller, faster, stronger, and meaner than me. Hurting me is too easy for him, and it has been getting easier the longer we are together.

"Answer me cunt! I should find something to shove down your throat so you have a reason to be so tight-lipped!" With Adam's anger morphing to rage so quickly, this will no longer be a quick smack around and move on. This is life and death.

"I'm sorry. I just had a long day and wanted to let off a little steam. I-I didn't know when you would be home." I slide my foot slowly to push the plug off the drain. If I'm going to die tonight, I would much rather have the ability to put up a fight. Drowning me will not be an option. As he gets closer to me, the stench of whiskey burns the inside of my nose and nearly gags me—wonderful, first anger, then rage, and drunk. "I swear, Adam, if you were home, I-"

"You would what, Lil? Cheat on me? Make out with some random dude at your little coffee shop? Show the world exactly who you are and how I will never be good enough for you? I am so sick and tired of your excuses. I bet you didn't even go to the bookstore. I bet you were whoring around like the slut you are! Don't think I don't know about your little fan page you have going on, too. I was kind to you by letting it slide. You should be kissing my boots." The air stills around me. I can't breathe.

"Oh yeah. I bet you didn't think I would find out about that one. Do you really think I'm stupid?" Before I can answer, Adam has hold of my hair.

The burning sensation of him dragging me out of the tub by the back of my head blackens my vision for a split second. I reach for his hands to rip them away from me, flailing every which way I can to make him let go. Digging my fingernails into his skin, the smell of iron peppers in the air. He will not get the satisfaction of me rolling over to take his abuse this time. "FUCK! I don't want to hurt you, Lil, but if you don't stop, you'll leave me with no choice!"

I throw everything I possibly can at him. I go to kick at his knees, but the wet tile works against me, forcing me to lose whatever hold I have on my own body and plummet to the floor. My head and neck are pulled upward as my knees slam below me, sending searing pain through my legs and deep into my hips.

Adam pulls my head back and shoves his face into mine until we are nose to nose. "Who were you fucking today, Lily?" If you want to be so close to me, let's see how you like this. I gather all the saliva I can in my mouth and spit in his face. Adam takes his free hand and wipes it away. A smile curls onto my lips as I glare at him with all the hate I can call forth.

Adam glances at his hand with disdain and draws it back, slapping me across the face with a force that makes white flash before my eyes. Through the ringing in my ears, I can almost hear him. "Fine, since you want to just fuck around with everyone, I might as well get in on the fun."

Adam grips my throat, making it difficult to swallow. I try to take a breath, but I can't. I can't breathe. Oh fuck, I can't breathe! Panic builds inside of me, taking over what little control I have left. "I need you to understand that this hurts me way more than it hurts you. I don't want to do this, but you leave me no choice."

My hands clap onto his wrist in panic to pry Adam's hand away my neck as the pull from my hair is released, leaving the pulses of pain to linger in its wake. My body is taking complete control over my actions as my mind is overwhelmed by pain. My muscles scream as my legs kick the best they can.

My vision starts to cloud inward. This is probably it. There's no coming back from this. The sound of a zipper echoes around me, and a new burning sensation starts between my legs. "Just like I thought. Soaking and fucking wet. You disgust me."

All the effort I had put into not succumbing to this vile man is futile. Everything I could have hoped and dreamed of was slipping away at his fingertips. I don't know if I'm still moving. If my body is still fighting. I feel so weak, so tired, so alone. "I love you, Lil, but if you're handing it out, I will get mine." This can't be real. He sounds so far away.

This is only a nightmare. My vision starts to tunnel. It has to be a nightmare. Come on, Lily! I know you can hold on for a little longer. Don't give in. Don't let him do this to us. The uninvited cool tears fall from my cheeks as he thrusts into me.

It's getting so dark. He won't get away with this. I won't let him. My chest jerks as my body attempts to take in a breath. I'm going kill him. Somehow, I will-

14

Samael

It's still early. I want to call Lily. Everything inside of me is screaming to do it. I believe in her. I know she can do this. If there was anything wrong, Levi would let me know. I can trust my team. After filling the dishwasher with the last of my dishes, I drop in a soap pod and head upstairs. I flick the light switch when I reach my room and fall face-first into my bed.

At least I have soft sheets. Some nights, this room feels so hollow. Every piece was picked for my complete comfort. Satin sheets, California king-size bed with memory foam, attached bathroom, and a gigantic walk-in closet with more room than I would ever need. *Ding Ding Ding,* I pull my phone out of my pocket and shoot straight up, seeing Levi on the caller ID. "What's going on?"

"I don't know, but it does not sound good, boss man. There was water, and then I heard someone walk into the house." I run down the stairs, grabbing my jacket and keys. "Next thing I hear is some guy screaming at her about being a whore, and well-" Levi hesitates.

I slam the door shut behind me. "Well, what, Levi?!"

"It sounds like someone is getting smacked around. I could be-" I hang up the phone and get into my car. Never again.

The leather heats beneath my fingers as I grip the steering wheel. Pushing the accelerator closer to the floor, the engine roars with anticipation. *"Hey, this is Lily. Sorry, I can't come to the pho-"* Fuck! Pick up the phone, Lily. This isn't funny! Pick up the fucking phone! The world outside blurs into streaks of color as I break every road law known to man. *"Hey, this is Lily. Sorry, I can't come-"* For fucks sake, woman. You need to answer your goddamn phone! *"Hey, this is Lily. Sorry -"*

Every time I glance at the clock, it doesn't move. My stomach feels as if it's doing cartwheels while the weight on my chest continues to grow. I should have never let her do this alone.

She would have been safe if I had just insisted on being present when she told Adam she was leaving. Now, she's all alone at that god-forsaken house with a menace to women that should have been eliminated long ago.

"Hey, this is Lily. Sorry, I can't come to the phone right now." This voicemail had better not be the last time I hear her voice.

This stupid car needs to go faster. Why won't you just go faster? Please. Please be okay, Goddess. I promise I'm on my way. Just hold on for a few more minutes. I'm almost there. I swear, I'm coming for you.

The car nearly drifts as I make the final corner to the house. If there is one thing I did right these last couple of days, it has been Levi getting me all the information he could on Lily. Among that paperwork was her current address. I'll have to remember to thank him when I'm through here. Smoke curls from the back of the car as I come to a screeching halt.

Forget closing the car door. Every second is precious and I just need to get in there. The number on the house is correct. Fuck it. I pick up my leg and kick at the front door. *BOOM!* "Lily, where are you?!" She doesn't respond even though I'm calling out for her. Where is she? The faintest sound of footsteps moves above me.

I sprint towards the stairs in front of me, jumping over Lily's purse that is laying scattered across the floor. "Lily! Answer me!" I know she is in this fucking house. Skipping every other step to get to her faster the edges of my vision turn red. There's water everywhere and... "Oh my God."

Out of all the horror I have seen living the kind of life I do, nothing could have prepared me to see this. Numbness comes over me, as I look at her twisted body. "Lily." My voice doesn't even sound like my own. Getting closer, I can more clearly see the mottled reddish purple handprint across her throat. My knees slam onto the wet tile next to her.

Lily, my sweet Lily. My Goddess. My everything. I should have been here. Tears well up as I lift my beautiful angel from the floor. The lump in my throat tightens, making it difficult to swallow. "Lily, Goddess, please wake up." I tenderly brush the damp hair out of her face revealing a swollen eye and bruising across her face.

I quickly scour the bathroom for something to cover Lily up with until I stumble upon a towel hanging on the door. My body trembles as I grab it and carry Lily into the hallway. She shouldn't be here anymore. I find the next closest room, lay her in the bed, and dry her off.

It's not until I reach her legs that it really sinks in on what has happened. So much blood and bruising. I clear my throat and cover her cold body with the blankets. Pressure grows in my jaw as my pulse rushes through my ears. I pick up her head, ensuring the pillow is under her comfortably, and gently kiss the top of her head. "I swear I'll find who did this, and I'll do things to him the devil would be ashamed of."

With a deep breath, I still myself, calling forth my shadows. Without hesitation, an empty void bubbles up, covering the floor. Emitting an indignant growl, they begin their search of the house. The void shatters, sending smaller versions of itself to flit across the rooms like a whirlwind of devastation. If he's still here, my shadows will find him.

"Reeeady ooor not. Here I come." I announce. The house shakes with each step I take, echoing the weight of my steel toe boots, as the sizzle of the wooden floor beneath my feet grows louder. He will know what terror feels like.

"Nope. You're not in the hallway." I say it in a sing-song sort of way. Taking my time, I crack each one of my knuckles. "Not in the closet." The void of my shadows stretches across the walls, showing me the path that directly leads to Adam. "Let's see, if you're not in the bathroom, or the bedroom, or the closet, and you didn't go downstairs; wherever could you be hiding?"

Steam leaves my flared nostrils with every exhale. The path to Adam grows darker as my shadows blanket it before me. The only light that remains emanates from my footprints behind me. I let my fingers stretch out, digging them into the drywall. The chalky material crumbles under the pressure as I rip through it slowly. "God told me what you did, Adam." The closer I get to him, the more clearly his mumbles become prayers. "He's not coming to save you like he promised. You broke his rules."

His breath is ragged, and the whispers of his shaky prayers

bring me so much pleasure. I can't help but laugh at him. "What did the big man say again? Oh, that's right. Rule number eight. Thou shall not steal." I stand deathly still in front of the door he hides behind. "You took something from Lily without her permission." *Tsk Tsk Tsk.* Reaching my hands out, I grab the doorknob and the tightly closed door. I lean into it, the white paint under my hand ignites quickly trailing across the face of the door. I lower my voice to a whisper, "I'm going to make you beg for death."

Within seconds, Adam's screams begin. A cruel smile grows on my face as I open the door, finding Adam crawling across the floor covered in what I can only assume is his piss. I instruct my shadows to rip his soul from him piece by piece. The shadows pass through his body one by one. Each time they do, Adam screams out in pain.

Tears and snot flow down his face as I watch him crawl across the floor away from me. "Please! Stop! God help me!" Consuming him would be a merciful act. I refuse to grace him with any. The smoldering footprints I've left behind grow into small flames that begin to eat away at the floor. With each scream I allow myself to embody my true form.

"You refused to listen to my Goddess, so in return, I will refuse to listen to your pleas." Smoke begins to curl into the room as the roar of burning wood becomes louder. Reaching out, I summon my shadows to raise his body into the air and bring him to me. They stretch out his arms to his sides and lock his legs straight below him. "Feel the torment of your savior. Writhe in his sacrifice for worthless humans like you." Blood begins to pour from the center of his hands and feet as my shadows drill into them leaving a gaping hole. Not enough suffering. He deserves more.

The house begins to quake with the rise of my hands. The wooden floor cracks and falls as a gaping hole grows beneath Adam's levitating body, allowing for the wails and screeching of tortured souls to resonate from it. A swarm of wasps flies into the room and surrounds his head. Their merciless stingers poke tiny holes in every available inch of skin, sending thin rivers of blood down his face. More. He needs to suffer more. Hurting me is one thing, but to hurt the people I love is unforgivable.

She was perfect in every way. The most beautiful woman I have ever laid eyes on. What we had was impossible. I never deserved her. I will never find anyone like her. Intelligent, kind, and a smartass all the same. The way her skin blushed with embarrassment. I'll never see it again. "Sam?"

Could it be? No, it can't be. She was so cold. Was she breathing? But she was ice cold. The world blurs, stilling as I see her standing there. Completely bare, shrouded in flames, my Dark Goddess. How is this even possible? She's right there. The warmth of tears singes my skin. "Lily….Goddess." I can breathe for the first time since I left her this morning. She's alive. She's alive! Lily takes a wobbly step forward, and I rush to her side. Before collapsing onto the ground, I reach out, breaking her fall.

"Shh. It's okay. I'm here. I'm here, Goddess." She can't stay here. She needs help. I have to get her to someone who can help. Lily's limp body is weightless in my arms. The roar of the flames consumes the house while I carry her to the car. She will never be alone again. From this day forward, I will protect her at all costs.

15

Samael

ne week later

She still isn't awake. I need to get to work and wrap up all this Cain crap. I'm glad that Manny took care of getting him out of prison, but this is not the ideal time. When She said my name, I couldn't move. I felt paralyzed. Lily standing there in the hallway, shrouded by beautiful flames. They wrapped around her body as if creating a shield.

The moment I get her to my house, I inspected every inch of her body, categorizing every injury. Burning them into my memory so that I will never forget the importance of listening to my instincts. This is my fault. None of this would have happened if I was just there.

It's in the past now. All I can do from this moment on is help her heal both physically and mentally. There is going to be so much damage control when she wakes up. Maybe I should get her a therapist. That would be helpful. No. There is no need to bring in more people into this situation. I will do it. I will help her through every step. If she wants a professional then I will get her one.

Some of the bruising has started to heal. Though I don't know what I can do to get her to eat. How long can she go without feeding? There are too many questions and not enough time. My phone vibrates against my pocket. It has been going off all morning. I just can't find it within me to walk away from her.

A hand squeezes my shoulder. "Let me take this watch," Hal says in a soft low tone. His lips stretch out to a thin lined smile. "C'mon, you know you can trust me. I've got this. The moment she stirs I'll holler for you." I don't want to leave her side, but I know I can trust Hal. If I let him stay here for a couple of hours, I can get some work done.

I rub my eyes and stretch as I get off the edge of the bed. "That's it getch'er body moving." Hal pats my back as I get up from the end of the bed. The only time I have left this spot was to go to the bathroom and change. Hal has been managing things while I've been away the best that he can, but unfortunately there are limits to his capabilities.

I get to the bedroom door and am frozen with fear of leaving her side. What if I can't get here in time again? The bed frame creaks as Hal takes my spot on the edge of the bed, grabbing one of the books I have sitting there. "I don't care if I'm on the phone with God himself. Yell for me if anything changes. I'll just be downstairs," I tell him.

Hal waves his hand in a shooing motion. "I will call for you. Now go." Hal demands. I take a few more moments and watch Lily's chest rise and fall before turning away, careful to leave the door cracked open behind me. As I start walking down the stairs, I hear Hal reading *A Tale of Two Cities* by Charles Dickens aloud.

I slide my phone out of my pocket and see I have an array of text messages and missed phone calls. I swipe them away and call Levi. "Finally! Took you long enough to call me. I heard the whole fucking thing. You're one scary mother fucker when you wanna be Sam. I'll give you that." I can't help but smile a little. It's good for him to know that I am not the type of person to mess around with.

"Yea, well, I've been preoccupied." I rub the back of my neck and head into the kitchen to make myself a cup of coffee. I can't remember when I last got a good night of sleep. "Give me the rundown on what has been going on," I ask while placing a wireless headphone in my ear so I don't have to hold onto it.

"Well the good news is that Hal did a really good job at keeping me up to date with what you're going through. Which, by the way, if you need anything just let me know. I'm happy to help you out. The bad news is I've been keeping an eye on Michael's surveillance team and found out that they lost Cain damn near completely after he was released yesterday." Levi clears his throat and pauses leaving enough space over the line for me to hear a humming and the sound of water pouring coming from his background. He must be in his aquarium.

Michael was well aware of what Cain is. I don't understand how someone so educated can be so naive. "Actually, I will take you up on that offer. I need you to buy Lily a new wardrobe. Her house burnt down unexpectedly and she has nothing left. Get her everything and send me the bill so I can pay you back." I grab the moka pot, unscrew the lid, and fill the base with water.

"I can do that. I have a friend on my Discord that works in fashion. Let me shoot her a message. Do you know Lily's sizes?" Shit, I don't off the top of my head. She wasn't wearing any clothes when I brought her home either for me to check.

I grab my tin of coffee grounds and open them up, pouring some into the filter. "Can you grab a picture of her from Saint Drogo's Roasters security camera and have her use that?" I really hope that will work. I would hate to have Lily wake up in the middle of me taking a measuring tape to her body. That is the last thing she needs.

"Yea that should work. I promise my girl can work miracles," Levi assures me. That was a close one. I close up the moka pot and put it on the stove to boil.

That takes one more thing off my plate. "Now, I'm assuming once you heard about Cain disappearing you began your own search." There is a long silence that comes over the phone. "Levi, tell me you started looking for Cain or have already found him." The pause draws out. I check my phone to make sure the call wasn't disconnected.

"I started looking for Cain or have already found him," Levi says in a squeaky voice. I slam my hands on the counter.

"Damn it Levi! You are literally my eyes and ears! How can you be so fucking thorough when I ask you to do a task, yet have no goddamn common sense to do things on your own?! We need Cain to get to Ali. Stop playing with your fucking fish and find him." I hang up the phone and pull my ear bud out. A knock comes from the front door. Who the fuck is that now?

I swing open the door and find a delivery driver at my door holding a large envelope. "Certified letter for a Samael Diovolos," the man says and holds out a device for me to sign. I grab the stylus and scratch my signature on it and hand it back. In return he holds out the envelope and I snatch it from his hand, slamming the door shut behind me.

The large white envelope is made out to me, but there is no return address. I flip it over and rip it open while I make my way back into the kitchen. I pull out a single piece of yellowed parchment and toss the envelope on the island table.

There's nothing on it. I flip it over finding "An eye for an eye." hand written in crimson ink. What the fuck?

16

Lily

Three Weeks after the incident

Some days, I feel like I left one relationship just to be in another. The last memory I have from that night is fighting for my life and then everything going black. The next thing I know, I wake up in a place I don't recognize. Everything hurts, and I couldn't scream even if I wanted to. My voice was so hoarse that it felt like glass was stuck in my throat when I tried to utter a word.

I'm glad that's over and I can finally talk again. I panicked that first week, but Sam was always there for me. Sam brought in one of those doctors who visit your home. I thought that was something of the past, but I guess they still exist. He prescribed me bed rest and some high quality pain meds. So, I stayed in Sam's bedroom primarily that first week.

I never knew they made a bed bigger than a king size. I feel like you can fit at least five Great Danes in this thing and still have room. The dark grey sheets are so soft, and the comforter has the right amount of weight, making it feel like a hug. There is even a master bathroom attached with a jetted tub. Other than the crippling guilt of having someone else take care of my every need, I wouldn't say being here is the worst thing ever. It's definitely the nicest.

Sam has gone over the top with my care, too. He said that I deserve the best. It's terrific, but pampering isn't something that I'm used to at all. A new wardrobe, my meals delivered to the room, every Epsom salt scent, fancy hair products, makeup, the list goes on. He even had Mr. M gather me some books to read if I felt like it. It's way too much, and I do not deserve all this. I wish I could repay him, but I don't know where to start.

Some nights in the beginning, I would just lay there in bed, twirling my hair or biting at my nails, unable to sleep or sit still, with this weight in my chest. I would find Sam sleeping in a chair next to the door, curled up on the floor, or even lying on the bench at the foot of the bed. Since he insists, I don't speak until my voice is healed like the doctor said.

Text messages have been the most significant help to talk to him. Well, that and charades. I've offered him his bed back, but he refuses every time. I've even offered him to sleep in the bed with me. He downright refuses to. Then, the night terrors started. So many nights, I woke up from one screaming, and he is always right there for me. It's happened more times than I would care to admit, and yet Sam hasn't complained once. I figured if he was in the bed with me, it would help calm me down.

Talk about a bunch of firsts. I've never been told no to having anyone sleep in bed with me. However, having someone scream in your ear every night would be difficult. I know he can see the disappointment on my face.

He tells me time and time again that he would be honored

to, night terrors or not, but I need to recover, and he doesn't want to wake me more than I already am. I don't believe him when he says the floor is more comfortable. It has to be me. Has he never slept in this bed? It is like lying on a cloud.

At first, it really pissed me off, but then when the night terrors turned into day terrors, I understood. Just last week, I didn't hear him walking behind me, and I went after him out of instinct. I don't know what came over me, I was so scared. Thankfully, he can take a hit from me. I felt so bad when I realized that I had punched him in the face.

A split second later, the fear of him surprising me transformed into fear that he would retaliate, and I ran to the pantry to hide. Sam sat at the door talking to me. Telling me ad nauseam that I am okay and safe. That he isn't upset. That he is willing to take all the hate and anger I have. I stopped bugging him about the bed after that.

The next thing I knew, the night terrors got worse. I keep dreaming that I'm standing in this black space. There are flames everywhere, and I can hear these screams. So many people were screaming. That thing starts to walk towards me. Its bony wings are massive, and instead of eyes, it has blue balls of flames. It's like a dark angel, terrifying and comforting all at the same time.

I was prepared for the nightmares of Adam. I can understand why I would have them. These dreams are entirely different, like some twisted memory that doesn't feel real. I haven't told Sam about it, and he never asks; he just accepts. It could be how my brain processes the information. I hope it is, at least. Otherwise, I have completely lost my mind.

After the second week, Sam had to get back to work. Something about an important case, and his client was getting off. When he left for work, Hal hung out with me. I think Hal and I are becoming close friends. It feels so blissful to have a friend again, besides Mr. M. He has told me so many stories about Sam. I don't have to talk much, either. Hal has so many life stories. He talks enough for both of us.

Knock Knock "How are we feeling today?" Sam walks into the room, and the sight of him makes my heart race and body warm. I'll never understand why he knocks to come into his own room. However, I appreciate the privacy. All of this is his. He can come and go as he pleases. I'm the guest.

"Pretty good. Most of the bruising is gone, and I don't sound like I smoked two packs of cigarettes a day for the last twenty years." His smile reminds the butterflies in my stomach that it's time to do their thing. Getting out of bed today is the smoothest my body has moved in a while. Before I know it Sam is in front of me with his hand stretched towards me. "I got it. I don't need your help." In true Lily fashion, my foot is wrapped in the sheets, and I start falling forward.

"Yeah, I can tell," Sam chuckles, catching me before I make it anywhere close to the floor. "You really can't keep yourself from falling for me. I think it's a sign." he winks as he flashes a wry smile. I hop on one foot, struggling to free the other one. Sam makes sure I'm steady before he frees me from the perilous clutches of satin.

"I can't help it. The sarcasm that falls out of your mouth every other sentence just really gets me going." I toss the hair out of my eyes and fix myself. "It's either that or all the food you've been forcing down my throat. I swear, I've gained at least ten pounds being here. I haven't eaten so much in my life," I groan.

Sam starts to make the bed. "Good, you need to put some

weight on yourself. Can't have my Goddess going anywhere looking as if I starve her. What kind of person would that make me?" He picks the bed sheets up and tosses them onto the bed haphazardly. My eyes drop to the floor. That would make him like every other man I've been with. What use am I if I'm overweight? Adam would belittle me anytime I would clear my plate. Told me that if I got any bigger, he would lock me in the room and starve me. He called me every name in the book.

I should have refused to eat so much. There's no excuse for indulgence. I'll have to cut back. Clearly, it was too much. Sam's gentle touch on my arm brings me back to reality. "Hey there. Don't get all insecure on me now. I just want you to be healthy. I'm sorry if I hurt you. I didn't mean to." I wipe away the stray tears from my eyes and shake off the memories.

"Forget it. It's nothing I can't fix." I take a big breath and force a smile. Sam's eyes get smaller, and his jaw tightens. The attempt to recover quickly is obviously futile. He brushes the back of his hand on my cheek.

"I need you to look at me, Goddess." The wet feeling on the palms of my hands gives me the excuse I need to fiddle with my shirt. Wiping them dry forces me to center as my mind threatens to slip away from the present.

"Please look at me," he implores softly. I don't want to. He doesn't understand. He isn't a woman. He isn't me. I doubt anyone has ever told him how he is supposed to look or track his calories. He could eat everything in sight, and no one would bat an eye. Sam gently holds onto my chin, forcing me to face him.

"There is nothing to fix. You are perfect in every way. I love that you are hungry and that I can take care of you. I love that you're obsessed with chicken nuggets. The way you moan softly every time you eat chocolate drives me through the roof. I'm honored that you let me take care of you. I want to satisfy your every need." He puts an emphasis on every need that makes me think he is talking about more than my actual health.

He places his hand on the small of my back and pulls me in. "I already told you I won't let you suffer. You're mine, Goddess. Forever and always, whether you accept it or not."

Sam wraps his arms around me. If only he knew the kind of monster that lays in his arms. I love him too much too soon. I can't survive just on him. I've proved that with Adam. I know how this ends. My eyes sting, and I bury my face in his chest. It doesn't matter what happens to me. I need to feed soon, and I won't let it be from him. I have to leave before I hurt him.

17

Samael

I fucked up. I should have kept my mouth shut about the food. I know that's a sensitive topic for any woman. Why would it be any different for her? After everything Adam has put her through, I can only imagine what she has dealt with her entire life. I have to figure out a way to make this up to her. With the sweet, sultry taste of her sins at the coffee shop, there was no hesitation in feeding her, and every day after that, the need still lingers. I crave her.

How do you explain to someone that you know what they are because you know you're something far worse? She needs to feed, and I'm willing to give her every last drop of my tainted soul to satisfy her. When I first brought Lily here, she was so weak. I didn't want to, but I had to treat her body first. The damage was so extensive. There were so many cuts and bruises. Her eye was swollen completely shut, and the blood. So much blood. She fought back. I know she did.

I think the stress of everything put her primal needs into some sort of hibernation. Still, once Lily started to mend on the outside, I was able to see that other part of her come back to life. I've stayed as close to her as possible without it sniffing me out. She needed to rest. That's what the first doctor said. Keeping my distance has been a living hell.

I just want to hold on to her and never let go. Be that security for her. She needs to know that she is finally safe. The first time I decided to say fuck it and crawl into bed with her, she tried to strip me down. That's how I knew she was getting better. I refuse to cross that line with her if she isn't entirely with me or consciously present.

I sent my shadows out to collect whatever desires they could for her. I had hoped that she would be able to consume what was collected the same as I could, but I was wrong. Night after night, I offered it up whichever way I could without crossing that line.

I went as far as having my shadows pass across her lips in the hope that her instincts would take over again and just eat. Unfortunately, nothing worked. I'm not ready to tell her who I really am and what I can do. It's too much for someone healthy to handle. Trying to explain it to her when she is healing… She wouldn't understand. It's too heavy of a cross to bear.

At least a dozen phone calls later, I finally found someone like her, well as close as I could get to someone like her. An Incubi that goes by the name of Asmodeus. Unsurprisingly, they're friends with Levi. That man has more contacts than I know about. I suppose that's what happens when you live a completely separate life on the internet. According to Asmodeus, there is nothing I can do to help her, but they knew of a few tricks that would help.

After a lengthy vetting process, I had them come to the house under the guise of a doctor, just in case Lily came to. She was in and out of consciousness so frequently I had to be prepared for anything. For all I know, Lily isn't even aware that there are more sex demons than just her in the world, hiding in plain sight. Asmodeus gave me an herbal mixture called Essence of Desire.

It's basically synthetic lust. With that, she would not only heal faster, but it would suppress the need to consume organically for a short time. Once it wore off, though, Lily would go completely feral. Asmodeus warned that there would be no stopping her. Now that she is better, I have to get her to them. I agreed I would. They have a safe location where Lily can eat till her heart's content and she is satiated completely. She needs to learn about herself and what she is capable of. I'm running out of time.

I pour hot water over the last bit of herbs and some Earl Grey with a small splash of vanilla. I've gotten into the routine of making her tea every morning while she gets ready for the day. She thinks I'm just really bad at making a London Fog. Once this is over, I'll invest in a frother. I think she will really like that extra flair. "Is that what I think it is?"

Before I can even give her the glass, Lily snatches it out of my hands and breathes deeply, gently sighing. "Only the best for my Goddess." As she takes a sip, I catch myself wishing how her lips were on me instead. If it wasn't so irrational, I would smash the cup for being the first thing to touch her lips in the morning. The little satisfied hum she lets out drives me mad. My hands ache to touch every inch of her soft skin. My pants start to constrict around my groin, sending a shiver down my spine.

"I think you're getting better at this. It's not as bitter as it usually is." I feign a smile. I have kept everything the same.

There was only a half a dose left. Asmodeus didn't tell me how much time we had before it wore off.

"Since you're feeling better, I was thinking we should go out tonight." Lily stares at me, placing her tea on the table. "I want to celebrate you and everything you are. We can do anything you want, or if you're up for it, I know of a place that I think you'll enjoy."

Lily stays quiet for a while. The anticipation for an answer starts to weigh heavy on me. I have to get her to him. This is the best way without scaring her. "Samael." My heart drops at her tone. She never calls me by my name. Why is she calling me by my name?

"I wanted to save this conversation for later. I don't know how to say this exactly. Since I am better, I think it's time that I go. I really appreciate everything you have done for me these last few weeks, but I don't think I should stay here any longer. I've overstayed my welcome."

"Please. I'll drop to my knees and beg you if I have to. Please don't." Knots in my stomach form at the thoughts of her following words. I knew I fucked up this morning. I should have never said anything. "I can't breathe without you. This life means nothing if you're not in it. Please. Goddess." The lump in my throat grows. "I swear you have not overstayed your welcome by any means. If anything, you haven't stayed long enough."

Lily shifts in her seat and starts to twirl her beautiful hair around her fingers. "This has already been a lot. Just know that leaving hurts me, too. What we have is something that I will cherish every day of my life. I wish I could explain the reasoning. Just trust me. You're better off without me."

She stands from her chair to leave. I can't lose her. I won't lose her.

"Try to explain it to me. Please. I need to understand. If I did something to offend you-" I take a step towards Lily but freeze as she steps back away from me.

"I'm not good enough for you. I'm broken. Used up. Damaged goods. You've done more for me than anyone in my life. I can never repay you. I'm not worth it." Her eyes grow glossy. This isn't happening. I can't let this happen.

"Don't you dare talk about yourself like that. You are perfect. You are not broken. I want all of you, Lily. I want the good and the bad. The ugly and the beautiful. Put your luggage down and let me carry it for you. There is nothing in your past that can scare me. I'll take it all. Let me take all of what you think is dark and love you anyway." The last of my pride falls to the floor with me as I drop to my knees. "Please. Don't go. Please. Stay. I love you, Goddess."

"It's better this way." She runs up the stairs. I won't let her go. My feet won't move fast enough to catch her before she makes it into the room. I stop breathing once I get to the door and see her packing some clothes into a plastic bag.

"Lily, please don't do this. Goddess, I'm begging you!" She doesn't even turn around to look at me. She can't. "Did you not hear what I said! I love you! This isn't better!" I rush up to her, watching as she moves from the closet to the bag with clothes.

"There's more to me than anyone can understand. You have a life out there, Samael. You have a career, friends, probably family, and I have none of that. Call it right person, wrong time if you want to, but the reality of all this is that I am not going to hold you back from all the goodness that you possess."

I grab the clothes she puts into the bag and throw them back into the closet. Every last piece. "Samael, stop it. I have to leave. For fuck's sake, can this get any more cliche?" She juts out her hip and pinches the bridge of her nose. "It's not you, Sam, it's me. Let me go."

"I understand you more than you know, Goddess. Let me prove it. Tonight. If I can't prove to you that we are worth it then you can go. I'll even help you pack your bags. Pinky promise." I hold out my trembling pinky towards her.

"What are you, twelve?" I stand there in silence. Seconds feel like minutes. Trust me, please. Please. I'll show you everything. I step closer to her, keeping my eyes locked on her, pinky still out.

She examines the room as if weighing her options and squares her shoulders. "Fine, tonight, and that's all you're getting." She wraps her little finger around mine, and I can finally breathe. Tonight, Lily will meet with Asmodeus, and then I will tell her everything. I'm going to tell her what I am. Then she will understand. I'll make her understand that we are made for each other.

18

Lily

I knew that I shouldn't have brought up leaving him. It would have been better if I just left without saying a word. I would have left a note or something, at the very least. His presence became so broken as the words fell out of my mouth. My heart shattered into a thousand pieces with every word. I have never had a man fall to his knees and beg me to stay. And then he said he loves me.

I want to tell him I love him too, but what good would that have done? Sam would have just tried harder to make me stay. It's because I love him that I have to go. I love him so fucking much that it makes me believe that soulmates are a real thing. It makes no sense. That first day at the coffee shop, it was as if an invisible force was pushing me towards him. For the first fucking time, I feel safe. All those things I've been searching for my entire life are right here in front of me, and yet, I can't have it. Fate is a cruel thing.

It doesn't matter what he said, either. I am broken. I'm the most broken soul on the face of the earth. The only hope I have that there might be more people out there like me is

Mr. M's monster book. Even there, it talks about how my kind is dangerous along with the rest of the other creatures. Talk about an icebreaker. Lily, succubus, also known as a supernatural sex addict.

I haven't fed in so long. I can feel it creeping back up. That burning need to consume another's desire. I want to understand how I've lasted this long with Sam around and haven't gone completely feral, but there is no use. I'm just going to chalk it up to stress and healing. It's the only logical explanation I can come up with. When Sam was staring at me in the kitchen, I could smell it on him. The intensity of his desires growing the longer I sat there.

I want to blame it all on not feeding. I just can't find a way to do that. The chokehold this man has on me, and all we have done is kiss. Every time I see him, my body heats up. I crave to feel him inside me. The overwhelming need to wrap my lips around him leaves me soaking wet. Every. Fucking. Time. The things I would let this man do to me would make a nun blush.

If I wait around any longer, I'm going to hurt him. It's probably not normal to just jump back into bed with someone so soon, but what other choice do I have. Besides, I am anything but ordinary. There is nothing natural about eating human souls and consuming their lust through sex. That is the type of thing that nightmares are made of or dreams, depending on who you talk to. I just need to make it through tonight, and then I'll be gone. Sam will be safer with me as far away from him as possible. There is no other way.

"Quick! I got the goods! Move ya ass, chicky. We have some shopping to do!" Hal's smile stretches ear to ear, waving Sam's credit card in the air as if trying to get the picture on it to develop faster. "Shake a leg! I need you to buy me this new comic book that just came out. Two words. Collectors. Edition." When I first met Hal, I would have never pinned him as a guy who still collects comic books and action figures.

"Why do I have to buy it for you? Doesn't Sam pay you to drive him around?" Yet, here we are. A whole-ass-grown man is excited to head to the comic book store like a kid on Christmas. Hal starts dancing around, swinging his arms and hips towards the door. As if his windmill arms would get me to walk any faster.

"Of course he does. He pays me incredibly well, as a matter of fact." The moment I reach the door, he gently nudges me forward, moving me out the door ever so slightly faster. "Give me a reason I shouldn't spend his money if he handed *me* his card?" Hal's mischievous energy is so contagious.

I dig my heels into the floor, Hal's big smile and wide eyes makes me giggle. I intentionally raise my eyebrow to match his playfulness. "On one condition."

"Yes, yes. I'll take you to see your beloved Mr. M. Can we go now?!" Satisfied with his answer, I grab Hal's hand and pull him out the door. Rushing the both of us out of the house and into the car at full speed.

If there is one thing I have learned about Hal, it's that he's never really grown up. With how he talks about his past, it's easy to see that the years have hardened him. When Sam is around, Hal is stoic and strong, like an immovable force beckoning you to try crossing him. However, when it's just us, the stress of work doesn't show. He's an entirely different person. There's a glimpse of happiness in his eyes when we hang out. True happiness. I don't know what happened to Hal. I just wish the world wasn't so cruel to him. Maybe then he wouldn't be so stiff all the time.

Before I can even realize where we are heading, Hal parks the car with anticipation. "Alright, I promise we will go to your bookshop right after this. I'll even carry your books for you." Stepping out of the car, I honestly am unsure what to expect. On the outside, the comic book shop appears like any other bookstore. "I've already called ahead, and they are holding me a copy. I have an in with the owner." Hal winks and drags me into the shop, acting as if we are on some sort of covert operation.

The moment Hal pushes open the door, it becomes painfully apparent that I am not their normal clientele. The silence that falls over the shop is deafening. Every eye turns to me. I grab my tits and act shocked. "Oh my God, how did these get here? Hal! What kind of magic is this?" I don't know who laughed harder, Hal or the rest of the people in this place. As the laughter dies down, the people inside move around the shop picking up flimsy paper books and quietly speaking among themselves.

The air shortly became thick with excitement. Now that I can look around, my eyes widen at the kaleidoscope of colors that pop on the shelves. Superheroes, mythical creatures, monsters, and more. Cautiously making my way through the aisles, I take my time to study everything. I've never been to a comic book store. I mean, I've browsed the manga aisle once or twice, but this is entirely out of my element. The longer I hang out here, the more comfortable I begin to feel. It's just like any other bookshop. This one just has a lot more pictures. With each step, I find a new adventure waiting to be read. The walls were covered with boxes of action figures and posters.

As I turn the corner to the next aisle, I hear the rustle of pages and the occasional burst of laughter from the patrons. It's a smorgasbord of culture and diversity, proudly displayed everywhere you lay your eyes. By the time I make my way back to the counter, Hal is holding a thin book wrapped in plastic. "Is that it?"

"Is that it? Is that it?! Lily, this is the first edition. Do you know how much you just spent on me? Have some respect for the holy grail that I now possess." He doesn't even look away from it as we head to the door.

It takes us only a short time to get to Mr. M's. I need to go through that book again and see if there is anything in it that will tell me how I can hold out for just one more night. Apparently, while I was M.I.A., Sam stopped by often, keeping him informed of my condition. The familiar sight of his shop eases some of my worries. Now that I know there is second account information on my condition, we can call it, I can learn about myself and what I can do.

The jingling of the bells, mixed with the comforting aroma of ink and aged paper, sends a thrill of anticipation through me. "Lily! Oh, Lily! I've missed you!" Mr.M moves faster than I have ever witnessed around the desk. I reach out, and we embrace in a hug. I think we both need this. "Let me look at you." Mr. M pulls back and scrutinizes my face. Wrinkles form between his eyes as he moves his body to see me from different angles.

"I'm alright, I promise." I twirl around and haphazardly wave my arms around. "See? All better." The wrinkles on his face soften lightly. "Before you get all mushy on me, I came to see if we can read that book again. I haven't stopped thinking about it since you first showed it to me."

Mr. M chuckles. "A little birdy told me that you were coming today." He winks. "I already have it out for us. I had a feeling you would be coming back. If I recall correctly, you were most interested in the succubus, right?" He walks to the table we always sit at and starts to flip through the pages of the tome lying on it. "Ah! Here it is! Succubi."

Meeting him at the table, I see the picture of the beautiful woman. "Thank you." His soft eyes bring a smile to my face. Now that I'm not skimming through it, I can tell it's been translated more than once. Small annotations cover the margins in various languages to include modern English. At least I don't have to struggle with Old English and whatever other languages are here. It's not that I can't, but this would take so much longer.

Demon

Origin: Unknown

Succubi seek out sleeping men, draining them of their blood, breath, life force, and semen. Preferring religiously minded men, the succubus will force them to have sex or will find their prey in their dreams. Having intercourse with them is how they drain men's energy. Avoid at all costs. Usually, succubi do not kill. However, they are intensely capable of it when provoked. No other ways can they be destroyed other than exorcism.

"Mr.M, is there any information on whether there was anything used to suppress their power?" He turns the pages, quickly reading over the text.

"Not that I can see here, but my mother used to tell me a story about a sigil. It's been so long that I can't remember exactly what it did. However, she would always say that it was incredibly potent against them." As he turns the pages, Mr. M points to a drawing at the top corner of the last page. "This one." With a swipe of my finger, I snap a photo of it. Finally, some good news. I take my time studying the sigil.

Both intricate and beautiful. Long sweeping strokes flowed in the center of a circle. Around it are three crosses. The embellishments within the book are gorgeous. "Do you remember the story that your mother would tell you?"

Mr. M leans back into his chair, taking his glasses off, and a smile grows on his face. "In the beginning…"

19

Samael

T hanks to Hal, I have a better idea of what Lily is looking for regarding jewelry. The trade-off was easy. He fills me in on what Lily gravitates to at the store, and in return, he can buy himself that comic he has been obsessed with. Why he never just bought it himself, I will never understand. It's a small price to pay to see her light up.

While they were with Mr.M, he told Lily about an old occult symbol, and she immediately became fascinated with it. She apparently won't stop asking if he knows custom jewelers or silversmiths. Thankfully, I know someone who specializes in the occult. Endora is the only person I know who will have something like this on hand.

So many people walk around calling themselves witches and have little or no power. That's not the case with Endora. She's the real deal. Over the years, I've worked hard to convince her to join me so we can finally end the war between myself and Michael. She refuses constantly.

Endora claims she is a Grey woman working in neither light nor dark, a true neutral. I made the mistake of threatening her mortal existence if she didn't join me many years ago when I first came here. I was so fueled by revenge. So stupid.

That was when I learned the true extent of her abilities. She could banish us all from walking the earth as mortal men if she really wanted to. I thought she was going to, but her threat was clear enough. I quickly realized that it was better to have her as much on my side as I could; as they say, The enemy of my enemy is my friend. She is the enemy to us all in the end; having Endora not hate me is a hell of a lot better than the alternative.

As I push open the heavy brass door of her shop, the bells hanging on the opposite side softly jingle. A mixture of incense and herbs thickens the air. Crystals of various hues, sizes, and shapes cover the walls. All kinds of different-themed tarot card decks, statues, and symbolic decorations spanning a millennia of religions are scattered around. I spot the statue the mortals have dedicated to me and can't help but chuckle. "I think it looks just like you." Power emanates from behind me.

"Do my eyes really look that goatish?" I playfully ask with a smile as I turn around. My gaze is immediately drawn to the origin of that raw chaotic power- A familiar elegant tall woman with skin like onyx and black curly hair, wearing jeans and a yellow tank top. Endora's cat-like eyes, one blue and the other dark brown, stare me down.

"It's been some time, Samael. To what do I owe the displeasure of your visit?" Endora crosses her arms over her chest. Clearly, she still isn't over the little show I put on for her. I deserve it. One day, she's going to like me. Hopefully.

"I was hoping you could help me with a little something." A flash of lightning reflects from her eyes. Okay, maybe this isn't the best way to start our conversation. I throw my hands up in surrender. "I swear. No funny business. I only want to see if you have something that someone very important to me is looking for." Reaching into my pocket, I pull my phone out of my back pocket, showing Endora the picture Hal sent me.

She swipes the phone from my hand, studying the picture carefully. "Someone important to you?" Without moving her head up, her eyes lock onto me as if looking over the brim of a pair of imaginary glasses. "I told you already. I'm not going to help." She goes back to studying the photo, using her fingers to zoom in and out.

I lower my arms. As I step forward, Endora straightens out and squares her shoulders. "All you're helping me with is to get something nice for the woman of my dreams. She likes old things, and who better to go to than my friend, who is the second most wonderful, beautiful woman on the face of this planet." I give her the biggest playful smile I can possibly muster.

"You have something brown right there," she sneers as she wipes the tip of her nose. This is going better than I thought it would. I've been here all of 5 minutes and I'm still not dead. That has to count for something.

"Do you have it or not? I really would much rather give you my business than anyone else." I persuade. Turning on her heel, Endora walks to the back of the store with my phone. Like a lost puppy dog, I follow along.

Stepping through the doorway in the back of the shop is like walking into an entirely different world. The dimly lit room has the heavy air of an otherworldly aura. Flickering candles cast shadows across the wet, aged logs covered in moss. My senses are overwhelmed when I feel my energy being seeped from me. It must be some sort of protection spell she put up. Good for her. She should protect herself.

"I think I might have something close to this, but I'm not sure if it's charged. You'll have to charge it if you want it to work." She stops in the next room, which is adorned with necklaces, rings, plump sachets, bones, knives, and so much more. The walls begin to feel like they are closing in on me as I step into the room with her.

"Why would I charge it?" I watch as spirits pass through the walls. Souls that have abandoned their afterlife in fear of judgment. Steadying my shallow breath is a task. This place is not for me. Just standing here takes effort. I can only imagine what would happen if anyone came back here uninvited.

Endora opens a chest and starts digging through its contents haphazardly. The clash of fine metal rings in the air. "It's a sigil of protection, depending on who is wearing it." Her arm reaches farther into the chest than seems possible. "This one is particularly ancient." She pulls out a small brass pendant and studies it closely.

"What exactly is it to protect you from?" I move closer to her and the passing spirits pause. Their hollow gazes penetrate through the veil of life and death. The room pulses with energy, nearly dropping me to my knees. Message received. Not moving any closer.

Endora pulls out another. "Here it is!" She wipes it off with the edge of her shirt and walks across the stone floor to me. "Honestly, I would have to study it more closely to be able to tell you that. It would take me a while. Artifacts like these don't come with an instruction manual, and the woman who gave it to me didn't say much."

She hands me the pendant and walks back out the door we

came. "Well, that isn't concerning in the slightest." I drawl sarcastically, following close behind her. This is the last place I want to be caught in. "I know you're not my biggest fan, but I think it's safe to assume we have a mutual understanding of self-preservation." Endora doesn't miss a beat as she exits the first room, back into her shop.

"I think we both understand that I don't need a silly little trinket to send you back to the depths of hell, Samael." Good point. When I fully enter the shop again, I feel all my power rush back into me. I knew that the wards were draining. I just didn't realize how weak they really made me until now. I would be absolutely helpless if I was trapped back there.

"Endora, I really don't care what happens to me, but I will stop at nothing if you hurt someone I deeply care about. Damn me every which way you can imagine, rip my blackened soul from this corpse, but you will leave my Goddess alone." I place the pendant down on the glass counter next to the register. I won't make the mistake of crossing her on her turf today, but my point must be made.

Seeing my rage, Endora's eyebrows raise as shock paints across her face. She grabs the pendant and holds it between her hands. "This is only because you have kept your end of the bargain." She closes her eyes and takes a deep breath, slowly blowing it out of her pursed lips.

The room swiftly fades to black around us. The only remaining light coming from the flickering lights within the glass case between us. When Endora opens her eyes, they no longer bear the resemblance of anything remotely close to human. A pair of golden orbs take the place of her eyes. With each blink, a ripple-like water floats across them. A violet light emanates around her, and the sound of wind rushes towards me. Endora speaks in layers as if multiple spirits are residing within her.

"As the heart and soul align,
dark creator more divine.
When the vengeful hand takes its hold,
fulfilling prophecies never told."

Endora takes a long, choked inhale, and the room's heightened magic fades back to its average level of protection and wards floating about. I look around the room, near panic. "What the fuck was that?" She places the pendant back onto the table, trying to compose herself.

"Prophecy, apparently." Her labored breaths become more apparent. "I told you this symbol was ancient. Whoever it was meant for probably hasn't been around for a long time." Yeah, not doing that one. I will not be giving the love of my life a cursed object, looking for some random person to fulfill an ancient prophecy. Last I checked, we aren't living in some fantasy world.

"I really appreciate you looking for this, but I will not be buying that." I push the pendant back towards Endora.

"Honestly, I don't blame ya." She takes the pendant, placing it in the glass case. "I can find something else if you-"

"I'm alright. I think I'll just head out. This has been magnificent. I think we made some real progress today here that is really going to spearhead an impressive friendship." Endora crossed her arms again, taking her usual defensive stance. I grab a business card and put it on the counter. "Why don't you call me if you find anything that is similar to this and is not so…determined."

I back away as slowly and comically as I can. I should hold

my composure right now, but we both need this laugh. Fuck it, I need this laugh. When I reach the door, I feign stupidity, searching for the handle. "I had a fabulous time, Endora. Lovely to see you."

Endora slowly shakes her head back and forth in disapproval. I pull one leg out the door slowly behind me when I grab it. A smirk forms on her face, and I hear Endora quietly chuckle. Win! I knew I could get her to like me.

When I make it entirely outside, I take a moment to breathe. What in the world did you find at Mr. M's, Goddess?

20

Lily

Being back at Sam's house feels weird after this morning's events. Just a few hours ago, I told him I was leaving, and he begged for me to stay. I want to, but it just can't happen. I'm too dangerous. Shopping could have been better as well. Hal and I spent most of the day after our book run looking for something that is formal enough for Sam's liking, but spending that amount of money made me feel sick to my stomach. I've spent most of my life scraping by and saving every last penny I have. If it wasn't for the succubus powers, I doubt I would have come into all the money I have now.

I don't understand how people do it. They can just look at something cute or fashionable and not care what the price tag says. Granted, my book addiction isn't cheap, but a book is a hell of a lot more affordable than half the places Hal made me check out. There was this one dress that was gorgeous, though. Long, black, with a deep v-cut, open back, and tiny crystals covering every inch of it. When the light hit it, the shimmering reminded me of stars twinkling in a clear night sky.

When I tried it on, I felt comfortable and sexy. My shoulders didn't seem too broad and it hugged my curves in all the right places. It was as if it was made for me. I have to know. I shouldn't. Flipping the price tag around my heart drops at the cost. Let's oh so, carefully take this off. There is no way I can spend that much money on a dress that I'm only going to wear once.

Hal tried to convince me to buy it. Despite his efforts, the dress found its way right back onto the rack. Besides, I have everything I need here. Sam had bought me a couple of dresses anyway. I told him he shouldn't, but it turns out he's terrible at listening to me when it comes to spending money. I'm really a simple woman. I would much rather have a guy spend time with me than spend money on me. Granted, Sam does devote time to me. However, I really do not like being lavished with gifts. It makes me feel as if I owe him something.

I want this fantasy to play out. Sam and I, together happily ever after. But fairy tales aren't real, and nothing happily happens in my ever after. I'm doomed to be forever alone or hurt the people I love. The trauma is real.

Unless I can get that symbol made into a necklace or something to keep me from hurting Samael. According to Mr. M's mother, it's potent against succubi. Maybe if I wear it, it will suppress my need to fuck every person that I come across. Or, at the very least, it will suppress my need to consume their desires. If that doesn't work, then I can make one for Samael. Now, all I have to do is find someone who can make it for me and test the theory.

"Alright, we can do this. We have no idea what the plans are for the night, but we can find something in this closet that will fit the occasion." I crack my knuckles and throw open the doors to the closet. As I flick the switch on the wall, the room comes alive. Open shelves and drawers cover most of the walls. It's obvious this was made as a closet for him and her. How long did it take Sam to move his things?

Adam's house was caught in a fire the morning after everything happened. I had absolutely nothing. Part of me wants to believe that Sam really wants to take care of me, and that's why he went out of the way to get me a whole new wardrobe. I pass his suits, which look like they have to be dry-cleaned and go to the array he selected for me. Looking at it all now, it was more than Sam trying to be kind.

Every article of clothing gives the impression that they were chosen carefully and with full consideration of both style and comfort. There are jeans, t-shirts, leggings, pantsuits, and dresses. More choices than I need or ever had. Now that I think about it, I realize that these are the nicest clothes I've owned in my life. Well, I don't really own them. Sam does. He's the one who bought them. It's only right that I also leave most of these when I leave.

He must have cleaned after I left as well. Every single thing that I tried to frantically pack is in their rightful place. I grab the cheapest-looking articles I can find. Now that I'm not in a hurry, I can actually pack instead of tossing it all into a bag. It doesn't take too long for me to gather enough to survive a week or two and carefully place them into grocery bags so I can just get them and go when we return from our date.

One by one, I look at the dresses, pulling the top contenders out and laying them on the bed with matching shoes. There are almost too many to choose from. I step away, head into the bathroom, and turn the shower on as hot as it can go. I can distract myself with a long shower and pick the best one after. That should give me enough time to reevaluate my choices.

I toss what I was wearing in the wicker basket by the door and slip into the steamy water. The heat feels so lovely. My muscles loosen up, encouraging me to close my eyes and take in the moment of peace. Swaying back and forth into the water, I find myself in a trance of silence and relaxation.

The rhythmic sound of the water spilling over me and steady, even breathing pulls me deeper inside my mental sanctuary. For once, I feel as if I can finally think straight. Better yet, there is nothing to think about. The sound of heavy footsteps walking up the stairs breaks the silence, forcing my heart to painfully bound deep within my chest.

I listen carefully to the tempo and force of the footsteps as they get closer to the bathroom. My body trembles as flashes of that night threaten to steal my temporary reprieve from existence. With a sharp inhale, the familiar taste of red wine passes across my tastebuds, tantalizing my senses. I'm okay. It's only Sam.

Focusing on the sensation of my breathing, I straighten out my back and look around. I see the bottle of shampoo, the bottle of conditioner, the loofa, the hose to the showerhead, and the tile on the wall. I can feel my skin, the water, my wet hair, and the bottom of the shower on my feet. I can hear Sam walking into the bedroom, the sound of the water hitting my skin, and my breathing. I can smell the chlorine in the water and that I really need to wash up. I can taste "Mind if I join you?" Sam deep gravelly cuts through my focus.

I don't even attempt to open my eyes as I listen to Sam walk into the shower with me. Knowing he's seeing me completely bare sends a slight tingle of joy trickling down my skin. I can sense him scanning my body. I lean my head back into the water and rake the water through my dry hair, giving him an even better view.

The taste of sandalwood and red wine finds its way to my tongue as his want for me grows. When my hair is completely wet, I turn the water down so he can be more comfortable. "Have you washed up yet?" The raspiness of his deep voice fills me with need. I slowly shake my head no. As he reaches his hand under the water, Sam grabs the faucet, turning the temperature all the way back up.

"Isn't it going to be too hot for you?" Sam continues to feel the water until it returns to my scalding temperature.

"No, now turn around." If I only have tonight, I'm going to enjoy every moment of it. I turn my back to him and hear the pop of a bottle opening.

"I can wash myself." I look over my shoulder at him as he pours shampoo into his hand. The floral scent of roses fills the air.

"I know you can, but I want to take care of you. This is one of the many ways I like to show appreciation for everything you are." He puts the bottle back in its place and rubs his hands together, lathering the shampoo slightly. I lean my head back for him, shutting my eyes. Sam gathers my hair off my back and starts washing it. His strong, gentle hands massaging my scalp melt away the last bit of tension from my body.

Every sensation is enhanced, solidifying my want for him. The need to lean back and be in his arms. The desire to bend forward for him to take me. The water moves across my body. The soap sluggishly rolls down my back, sending tingles of pleasure through me. As he massages the last of it from my hair, I internally beg him to pull it just a little.

I hear the click of the shower head being put back into its rightful place and the pop of another bottle. The silkiness of the conditioner throws me into a state of submission. He has complete control. I want him to take it. Use me as his plaything. "Don't move." A heaviness settles into my chest. I hear him step out of the shower, open a drawer, and step back in.

Frozen in place, Sam spins my hair around, collecting it at the back of my head. I feel the familiar scrape of a hair clip on my scalp. A small whimper escapes my lips at the pressure building between my legs. Before I can turn around, Sam grips my hips and coaxes me out of the water.

The gentle scraping of the loofa moving across my breasts coaxes my desire to the surface. Sam's face is so still with unwavering focus. The care he takes smoothing over my curves like that of a painter as suds coat my body. Water cascades off his shoulders, defining every arch and slope of his rugged shape. It takes everything in me to not pull his face closer to my pussy as he kneels down. I prop my leg up on the small foot shelf, hoping he will take me for his own.

Sam chuckles, steady streams of water fall on his face. His bright blue eyes steady as Sam begins to run his hand up the length of my leg focusing intently on my skin. Sam's eyes darken as he cups my pussy with his hand as he slowly stands upright. "Please." I beg breathily. My eyes close as the whimper of need escapes me.

The added warmth and pressure from his hand threatens to make my knees give out. "Not yet, Goddess." His mischievous smile taunts me as he adds more pressure, skimming his fingers in between my folds. A whimper of want escapes my lips. "I'll worship you properly soon, but first-" I melt entirely as he takes his fingers soaked with my desire and licks them clean. "We need to finish getting you ready for our big night." Mother Mary and Joseph, this man.

21

Samael

Fuck, she tastes so sweet. I step out of the shower to keep myself from taking her right now. I need to be close to her. Everything about her pulls me in. Her long chestnut hair. Her sexy, beautiful doe eyes. The curve of her spine and how she arched ever so slightly when I was washing her. The way she commanded the shower, propping her leg up, offering herself to me.

I grab my towel and dry off quickly so that way I don't soak the floor. Carefully, I wrap the towel around my waist in a way I can keep my cock from tenting it. I need to get some briefs on. At least then, I can hold this thing back a little. The water in the shower turns off. Lily steps out of the shower, her soaking wet body highlighting each of her lascivious curves. Fuuuck! It's taking everything in me to not wrap my mouth around her tits. I would dry her with my tongue just so I can claim every last inch of her body. "Is there something wrong with me?"

Her broken tone derails my train of thought. "Why would you think that?" She watches me with puppy dog eyes as if she is begging me for some sort of reassurance, covering herself with her arms. I grab her towel and wrap it around her shoulder. "Goddess, there is nothing wrong with you. You're perfect."

I wrap her in my arms tightly. The congested sound that emanates from her breaks my heart. I was so fucking lost in my own goddamned head I didn't even notice she was crying. "There must be something wrong with me. I thought you-" she cries incoherently "- and we would, ya know. But you didn't. It's because of what happened." My body heats up. That motherfucker is still tormenting her, even when he isn't here. He deserves more than what I was able to do.

I gently lift her chin so I can see her face completely. Tears stream down her reddened cheeks. I can tell she's trying to hold her emotions back. "Goddess. It is I who should be apologizing to you. I should have never touched you without your permission. I have failed you most fundamentally. You didn't give me your explicit consent, which is unacceptable."

Her brows pinch together slightly. "I didn't tell you no. I didn't tell you to stop. You didn't do anything wrong." Her tiny humphs shatter me.

"But I did. I should have asked you if I could touch you like that. I should have asked. That's the bare minimum, and it didn't even cross my mind. You, my Goddess, deserve better."

She pulls out of my arms, wiping her face with the towel. "Deserve better? This is the best it's ever been! You have been kind to me for no fucking reason. Most men would have run away the second they heard about what happened to me. Nobody wants a broken woman. Nobody wants to deal with this sort of baggage." Lily points to herself with tear filled eyes.

"Yet there you are. Standing here. Apologizing to me

because of what? I damn near served myself up to you on a platter, and YOU said no." she slams her pointer finger into my chest. "YOU said not now." Lily steps closer, closing the gap between us punctuating her words with another forceful poke.

"So if YOU need my permission to touch me, then god-damnit, touch me! I want you to touch every inch of my body. I want you to do things to me that I can't even imagine or recover from." Lily removes her finger from my chest, her body trembling like a leaf. "Ruin Me." she she demands through gritted teeth.

Holy shit."No, I won't ruin you." I bark back. Lily's eyes widen, and her jaw tenses. "I refuse to even attempt to ruin you. I don't make it my business to ruin the people I love." I stand tall teetering somewhere between rage and protectiveness. Her mouth opens slightly. I think, for the first time, she actually heard it. Love.

"I don't call you my Goddess because I want to ruin you. I crave worshiping you. I want to build you up so that you can become the best version of yourself." I close the gap between us completely, standing over her and letting out just an inkling of my aura. "I will spend the rest of my god-forsaken existence fulfilling every one of your desires, but not until we have a conversation first. So get in that bedroom, sit down, and talk to me." I point to the door maintaining complete eye contact. "Tell me everything you want me to do and all the lines you refuse to cross. I hold myself to a standard, and this is it. Tell me how I can most satisfy my Goddess." I drop my hand and refuse to look away.

I won't be the first to break. There is a fine line between dominance and being an asshole. I choose the latter. If she wants me to take control then so be it, but I will not cross this line. I chose not to take what I want, and what I want is her submission given freely, not because she feels it's her place.

Without hesitation, Lily walks into the bedroom. I follow close behind her and watch as she plops herself onto the bed and starts pouting. "I don't understand why we have to go through a stupid checklist just to screw." This woman. I swear.

"Because not everyone likes it in the ass. I'm not a fan of it, are you?" I make my way over to the walk-in closet and grab a pair of briefs. As I bend down putting them on, I spy plastic shopping bags full of clothes hiding in the corner. She's ready to leave.

I pretend to not see them and grab my robe, handing it to Lily. "I mean, yeah. Under the right conditions. You've done anal?" Lily asks meekly. She drops the towel and puts my robe on. The satin red fabric wrapped around her body takes my breath away.

"Yeah, I don't mind it. I need a warm-up before I'm ready, though, and the right lube because otherwise, it's not as enjoyable as it should be. Honestly, I much prefer giving it than receiving it." Heading back to the closet, I start to move hangers around searching for the outfit I've chosen for tonight.

"So you've been with men?" Lily's higher pitched tone is questionable at best. This is where it all tends to end. Not many women I have been with like the idea of being with a man who has been with men, except for the occasional femdom. They hold a precious place in my heart.

"And women, is that a problem for you?" I clear my throat in hopes that it covers up the mild quake in my voice.. I peek my head out of the closet. She's sitting back on the bed, twirling her hair between her fingers.

"Not at all. It's like seeing a unicorn in real life." The tightness in my chest relieves itself. This could have gone an entirely different way. Succubus or not, she is allowed her opinions and preferences.

"What does a unicorn have to do with me sleeping with men? I think the horn is in the wrong spot, Goddess." A chuckle escapes me. I grab a white button-up shirt, black dress pants, and suspenders.

"No, I mean, it's rare to find a guy who is comfortable with admitting that." I finally locate the rest of my outfit for the night and hang it on the bathroom hook. She may need time to get herself together. The less space I take, the better it is for my Goddess.

We spend the next few hours talking. Really talking. Eventually, we get around to discussing what we both like and don't like. Things we don't even want to try. We cover just about everything I can think of. I did plan to take us to dinner, but because of how long we spent talking, we will have to settle for something at the club.

As I finish buttoning up my white shirt, I hear her gasp. A smile creeps onto my face. She must have finally found it. Hal had told me that she fell in love with a dress when they were out. A black one that was covered in some sort of stone. I had him grab it for her when she wasn't paying attention. When I got home, I snatched it from its hiding spot and put it in the closet for her to find.

As I sit down to put on and tie my black dress shoes, I glimpse her walking out of the closet. My eyes slowly follow Lily's curves from the ground up. Hugging her body like a second skin, the dress makes her shapely hips pop that much more. As I make my way up past her navel, more and more skin peeks through the widening gap made by the v-neck. Her breasts barely hold on for dear life, threatening to reveal themselves entirely at any moment. My body warms, and the blood flow that was heading to my brain is completely redirected. "Goddess."

She leans against the doorway, sliding her arm up. I sit up and enjoy the show she puts on for me. This is truly just for me. "How does it look?" she asks in a lascivious tone. Her eyes, both haughty and innocent as she slowly smooths the dress down her body. I feel like one of those cartoon characters whose eyes bulge out of their head watching her. I stand up and adjust myself. The room available in my pants has become significantly less all of a sudden.

"I think it would look better on the floor." I walk over to her and push her flush against the wall. "I want to kiss you, but I don't want to ruin your makeup. You worked so hard on it." She grabs me by the back of the neck and pulls me in. The tart cherry taste of her lips is intoxicating. I push my body further into her, taking hold of her waist. She pushes her hips into me, and I break away from our kiss.

"Not yet, I promise." I cup her cheek in my hand. "Soon. Just hold out a little longer for me."

22

Lily

I hate that I agreed to wait until later, but when I look into his eyes, the love that is reflected settles me. It's the least I can do to give Sam some closure. This monster within me wants me to jump on him and ride off into the night. Though, when I'm with him, it's as if he can see right through it and really see me. Every brick I lay down to build that wall, he takes two. Tearing it down, piece by piece.

I can almost see the future we could have if I stayed. The house, the luxury, hell, maybe some kids. Actually, scratch that. I'm nowhere close to ready to have kids. When I'm with him, the world has so many possibilities, and I'm free to explore them. No longer chained to the tortured past that has always been. He's kind. He's safe. He's home. I want to be home.

I let the weight of my head fall into his hand. With each swipe of his thumb, I can feel my defenses crumbling. The muscles across my shoulders relax more and more as the seconds pass. I wonder if he can see how much I want to stay, to be with him. It's a delightful dream, although I'm not a princess, and this isn't some fairy tale that has a happily ever after. Sam's brows pinch together slightly. "What's wrong, Goddess?"

It's then that I'm aware of the warm tears falling down my face. I almost want to wipe them away, but for the first time in a long time, I'm not crying out of sadness, fear, or anger. "Nothing. I'm just-" Sam pulls me away from the wall into his embrace. "-happy." I nuzzle my head into his shoulder and hold onto him. This may be the last time I can ever feel this kind of love. I want it to last for a little while longer. I coil my arms around him a little tighter.

Just a moment more.

Please.

Let me enjoy this peace.

Seconds feel like minutes. I let the tears fall. Now, I think I'm starting to understand. Water is cleansing. These tears were necessary for my soul. As each one falls, I realize. When I woke up this morning, I was so confused and lost. Yet, there was still peace. Watching him in the kitchen, I felt determined to do what I have to do. I don't feel that determination so much now.

I feel like nothing can stop me. "Shhh. I got you, Goddess. I'm not letting go." As he pets my head, I almost want to believe that nothing can stop me from achieving this Hail Mary. The flame of hope in my soul burns a little brighter. In his arms, so close that I can hear the steady beat of his heart. Nothing feels out of reach when it comes to us. Not when it's from the heart, and I'm shrouded in his love.

Slowly, I pull away. Ending this moment that will be etched in my memory for the rest of my life. Sam wipes away the last of my tears and gently kisses me. It's not a forceful kiss full of fire and passion. It's soft and dainty. I love you, Samael. I love you more every moment we spend together. If only this wasn't goodbye. "Do you want to fix your makeup?"

I nod and go to the bathroom. Seeing myself in the mirror, I know why Sam asked. I look like a raccoon. I grab my things and fix the mess I created. When it finally is all off, I just stare. Losing myself in my own eyes. There's a shimmer of that hope, but it is shadowed by the sharp sting of impending loss that I feel clawing its way through me. This is my war, and I must prepare for battle. I force myself to shake off these emotions and stand a little straighter, grabbing my makeup. I carefully place my armor. Tonight, I live for us.

Sam walks into the bathroom as I finish applying my red matte liquid lips. He stands behind me and I can see his eyes focusing solely on me in the mirror. "Beautiful." He wraps his arms around me again, resting his chin on my shoulder. I can see the soft smile showing itself. "I hope you enjoy what I have planned for us tonight."

* * *

Tonight, Sam decided to drive us. He takes us out of the city and drives near the countryside. Buildings are quickly replaced by tall evergreen trees. The street lights grow further apart until there are none. The only signs of civilization are the telephone wires and the occasional dirt roads I can catch in my sight. It takes about forty-five minutes before he starts slowing down.

I can only assume we are close as Sam slows, turning onto a gravel road. A small sign appears in the shape of an apple reading *The Forbidden Fruit*. I've never heard of this place. I have no idea what to expect. Where is he taking us? I turn down the music so I can see better. I am not sure how that makes sense, but it helps. The dense tree line begins to thin out around us.

Whatever this place is, they really do not want to be found. "Where are we?" I lean forward in my seat a little, the seat belt tightening on my waist with every adjustment I make. As we dive further down the path, tiny lights twinkle in the trees around us.

"Somewhere you can truly be yourself. However, you need that to be." I want to look at him, but the sight before me is enchanting. The few trees that line the road have grown in a way that makes it seem we are in a tunnel surrounded by fairies. I feel like I've been transported back in time or to some mystical land. When we reach the end, Sam turns into a filled parking lot.

He quickly finds a spot and parks the car. As the engine quiets, there is nothing but the sound of a fall night. Sam gets out, breaking the silence with the gravel rubbing underneath his shoes. I unbuckle, and my door is opened. Sam reaches his hand out to me. "Goddess." I hold his hand and step out of the car. He closes it behind me and gives me one of his classic mischievous smiles.

"There is one more thing you need to complete the outfit." Sam reaches into his jacket and pulls out a small intricate mask illuminated by the faux torch lights in the parking lot. Red jewels shine across it, filling the seemingly empty spaces as if they are holding the fine black lines together.

"Why would I need this?" I extend my hand to take it, but Sam pulls the mask away. He steps behind me and places it on my face. The fabric is lightweight and delicate. It covers just around my eyes and the bridge of my nose.

The ribbon hardly makes a sound as he ties it on. "Trust me."

He moves my hair out from under the ties and steps around. Somehow, in the short time of him putting my mask on, he donned his own.

Black, sharply pointed horns curl up from his forehead. Its red material matches the jewels of my own. Black highlights trace along his face, exaggerating his cheekbones with a sinister flair. The faux flames of the lamps flicker and dance across him, bringing his mask to life. Yearning builds within me, and so does my hunger. When I told him once I was into masks, I didn't realize I am this into masks. Forgive me, Father, but I'm about to sin.

We follow the winding path towards my surprise. As we make our way around the corner, I'm drawn towards a magnificent stone castle standing amidst the darkness. It's undeniable grandeur takes my breath away. The castle is illuminated by a soft, fiery glow from the light fixtures it is adorned with. Each window sparkles like a beacon of light. A single candle can be spotted in each one.

I need to catch even the slightest glimpse of the land. The expanding grounds are meticulously landscaped, the lush greenery accentuated by the soft moonlight filtering through the branches of towering trees.

Sam takes hold of my hand once more and wraps my arm around his. Guiding me to the imposing doors that stand tall at the entrance. Men in fine black suits stand on each side of the path like statues, each wearing matching simple flat white masks. The crisp fall air gently blows behind me. The doors looming open before us as if inviting us inside to witness its magnificence.

I grip onto Sam's arm a little tighter hoping my palm doesn't sweat and stain his sleeve. With a single step, we pass the threshold. Within a few strides, we are met with a vast marble staircase. A woman in a suit that matches the men outside steps forward. Sam slips off his jacket, takes my coat off, and hands them to her. She gives him a small ticket, which he slips into his wallet.

My breath is stolen by the majestic structure. "Are you ready?" I don't know how I can be ready. I am not prepared for something like this. This is a place people like me dream about going to. The type of house that makes you want to live out the childhood fantasy of running through it in a ball gown at full speed.

Without reservation, I push forward. Sam leads me up the stairs. Reaching the second floor, sizable wooden doors appear on both sides. How have I lived here my entire life and never knew there was an actual castle? This must be one of those hidden gems where you have to know someone to even find out about it.

A set of oversized oak doors open for us as we approach it. There have to be cameras in here. There is no other way; their timing can't be this good without them. The dark, flowy fabric inside the door covers what lies ahead. As we get close to them, one by one, the panels fold up, allowing us to pass through seamlessly. Crimson light filters through the final curtain. As it rises, a sight I am both familiar and unfamiliar with is revealed.

A bottomless hunger bubbles to the surface. The smell of leather and sweat assault my nose, driving what little self-control I have left to the brink of extinction. Electricity curls up my spine. I. Need. This.

23

Samael

Iknew coming here was a gamble, and it appears that I've won this round. The Forbidden Fruit is more impressive than I expected. Asmodeus knew precisely what they were doing when they made this place. Damn, nearly every fucking inch of The Forbidden Fruit is filled with people and sex toys.

Lily purrs as she takes in the sights before us, a sound that I never heard from her before. She transforms into an image of visceral temptation. Pressure builds in my groin as her spine twists upright, and she rolls her shoulders back. Her movements are slow and purposeful. She lifts her chin slightly, commanding the attention of every person who chooses to look our way.

"Tonight you feast, my Goddess." Lily's eyes darken as her lips curl seductively. I take her by the arm again. Before I let her go to get her fill, I want to walk around and see what she wants to enjoy.

Lily doesn't hesitate to take the lead, walking through the crowd in front of us. This place is a succubus haven. Every type of sexual act and accessory you can possibly imagine is placed artistically throughout the massive room creating a sensual, seductive space for one to enjoy all the pleasures of the flesh. Each section of the entertainment floor seems to be dedicated to a different kink. The crack of the whip commands my attention.

The sharp sound catches my Goddess's attention as well. She walks us straight to a naked woman in a deep purple mask lying on her stomach, ass up. A muscular man wearing black dress pants and matching corset swings back a wooden paddle with holes drilled into it and smacks it across her left cheek. As we get closer, we can see the woman is wearing a ball gag in her mouth and chains on her wrists that tether her to the spanking bench. The woman lurches forward, crying out from the sting of the paddle with each strike.

When we walk past the tables, our path is interrupted by a man wearing a full-face latex mask stretched out across a table. The first man lies prone while someone else, their body encased entirely in leather, runs a violet wand over his body. The wand travels in swirling patterns before pausing at the tip of his partner's dick. His moans have started attracting a crowd. Lily only stays for a short time, and I can do nothing but follow like a lost puppy.

Her pace picks up. This place is making her come alive. The way Lily sashays her hips and plays with her hair makes it obvious that she is well within her comfort zone. There are no limits in this den of carnal sin.

We pass a few tables that are being used for refreshment breaks. Some have people sitting and enjoying food and drinks, while others remain empty. We come across a table with a woman lying on top of it, seemingly serving herself as a meal. The fingers of her left hand twist restlessly in the confines of her long black hair as the other skims over the contours of her lushly appointed body, every curve highlighted through the sheer fabric of her short red dress. As we approach, she turns her face to us, almond shaped eyes widening at the sight of Lily prowling closer.

Lily lets go of my arm and confidently stalks her prey, hips swaying. She gets close to the woman's face while brushing her disheveled hair from her shoulders. I can't hear what she says, but I know precisely what will happen by how she leans over her and smiles radiantly.

Lily slides the straps of the woman's dress down slightly, guiding the woman's arms out and allows the bodice to gather in the woman's lap, baring her chest. As Lily makes her way to the opposite side of the table, the woman pulls her legs out of the dress and hands it to my goddess, spreading her legs open. Lily drops the dress and I watch as it floats to the floor.

I wet my lips, hungry for my Goddess. She needs this more than I do. She's starving, and I know it. Lily runs her hand up and down the woman's legs. She curls her hands around the woman's hips and pulls her closer. Lily then grabs the woman's knees and slowly drags her tongue across the woman's dripping wet pussy. The woman inhales sharply, and Lily begins to feast on her like a feral beast who has been starved.

The woman on the table arches her back and grips my Goddess's head for dear life. With her other hand, the woman reaches for me. I grab hold of it and then take control of the other, keeping her in place. I knew Lily was wicked. Good Girl. I can't take my eyes off her as Lily slips her fingers deep into her meal. Fuck. Keep going, Goddess. Get every last drop.

With the sound of the woman's orgasm breaking through, Lily climbs on top of her, moving closer to the woman's face as if to devour the sounds of pleasure. A faint blue wisp materializes from the woman, floating for a second in between them. Lily takes the light in her own mouth as she kisses the woman. Lily purrs once more, though this time deeper and more primal. A flash of light shines in Lily's eyes as she lets the woman go, hopping off the table, and moves deeper within the club. I quickly follow and adjust myself.

My temptress is a Lion amongst lambs. Stalking around the shadows of this den of sin. Taking precisely what she wants when she wants it. I couldn't be more proud of her. I follow behind at a distance this time. Watching her consume meal after meal. Suffering internally, waiting for her. I want her to get her fill. She needs to. The pressure in my groin is starting to become painful.

My Goddess walks past a couple of masked men stretched out and chained to the wall. She makes her way into a nearby room off to the right. There are already six people inside, both men and women, in various states of undress. Lily's entrance parts them like the sea, revealing a queen size bed on a dark canopy bed frame in the center of the room, dressed in red satin sheets.

Lily confidently unzips the side of her dress and slips out of it, letting the garment puddle on the floor, leaving her bare. The prolonged anticipation is nearly unbearable, as she glances around the room seductively while stepping onto the bed and kneeling in the center. Lily turns to the three men standing closest to the bed, her long chestnut hair cascading down her chest.

She tilts her head with a nod and the nearby men ambush her. I step into the room behind Lily, sending a shadow out to collect the sins of the men with the intent to consume and evaluate the depths of their transgressions. None of them have the peppery burn of violence towards women. With Lily safe, there is no reason for me not to enjoy the show.

Lily leans down and rests her hands on the mattress, perking her ass up and spreading her legs, I find my way to a chair in the corner of the room. Eagerness grows within me as I watch a tall, athletic-looking man with warm beige skin, wearing a skeleton mask grab himself and tentatively massage his thick shaft in long strokes, making it hard and dripping. He gets behind Lily and slowly eases his erection into her. Once he is completely sheathed, Lily gasps and throws her head back in ecstasy as he begins to thrust. I want to fill her mouth with my own cock.

As if he could read my thoughts, a powerful looking man in an intricate silver mask moves into position in front of Lily. Deftly, he removes his boxers to reveal the entirety of his sun kissed physique as well as an impressive hard on. With one smooth motion, he quickly fills her mouth as well as sating my own unspoken desire. His muscular ass flexes with each thrust, muffling her moans and glistening with her saliva. Lily matches his urgency with her own lusty, unsated needs allowing her body to bounce carelessly between them.

Another man, pale and muscular, joins in by settling beneath Lily, his gaze eager through the holes of his white half-mask. I can see the crispy brown hair of his chest brush against her creamy skin as he slides into place, his large hands immediately reaching for Lily's ample breasts, firmly squeezing them, and sucking on them. His dick gets harder as he twirls his tongue around her nipples. Instinctively, her chest drops towards him and she stretches her neck, allowing for the outline of the silver masked man's cock to bulge with each thrust as it moves in and out of her throat. I can't help but stare desperately at the half masked man's curved rod bouncing with need, wanting to take it for myself.

Even in the thralls of pleasure, Lily doesn't take her sultry eyes off of me. I lean back into the chair and unzip my pants. Despite all the attention her body is getting, it's me who has her focus. The men rotate, each taking turns giving every inch of her body some of their attention. I pull my dick out and stroke it slowly, all the while maintaining eye contact with her.

Lily's teary eyes stray from my eyes and onto my dick, her body flushing, glistening in sweat. I pace each of my strokes with the man who is in her mouth. By the way her lips curl around it, I know she imagines it is me. "Eyes on me, Goddess. This is all for you."

The one in the white half-mask who is now behind her keels over, chasing his orgasm. She shakes her ass slightly and slowly milks out every last drop. Adding more pressure to my own strokes, I want to follow suit. As he pulls himself out, a man in a wolf-like mask takes his place. "You're doing such a good job getting yourself ready for me, Goddess." She frees her mouth and smiles devilishly at me.

"Come join," Lily breathily demands. I stand up, walking closer to the bed. Lily reaches out to grab me, and I step back just out of her reach. Her chest falls to the bed.

Nobody in the room loses their pace. Adjusting themselves to her movements. "I enjoy watching you get every single one of your tight little holes filled," I declare. Lily lets out a powerful moan of pleasure as another orgasm rolls through her. An idea sparks. I get the attention of the wolf-masked man behind her.

We make eye contact. "Harder." He grabs her hips, slightly rippling her skin, giving me a tight smile. Clearly, this isn't his first time being instructed. Slowly, he pulls the length of himself out and slams himself back in with a grunt. Her body jolts forward with each thrust. I put my dick back into my pants and zip it shut. Anything for my Goddess.

A little gasp comes from behind me. A thin pale woman with blonde hair and a golden mask is watching us from the doorway, eyes full of lust. "You." I point to her. "Come here." She walks into the room without a word, quickly stripping down as a blush blossoms on her pale skin. I survey the other men in the room, carefully examining each for a potential new participant.

One gentleman in particular piques my interest. His body is stiff as if he's nearly on the edge of losing control. His sin of fornication is so thick that I know he will give my Goddess more to eat. I beckon him toward us with one finger. He quickly complies, his eagerness bringing a smile to my lips as I instruct, "You pick her back up on her hands and fuck that greedy mouth of hers."

He doesn't hesitate to join in. He guides my Goddess back onto her hands. His brown skin stands out in stark contrast against the ivory silk of Lily's shoulders. "He's big, Goddess. Do you think you can handle it?" She opens her mouth completely, sticking her tongue out. The man behind her thrusts again, jutting her body forward and filling her mouth with the cock in front of her. Her eyes fill with determination at his size. "Grab her by the back of the head and slowly fuck her face." I point at the man behind her, "You fuck that pussy so hard that she has no choice but to gag on this cock."

I feel like an artist who is orchestrating the perfect scene. The woman taps me on the shoulder, pulling my attention from the bed. "Crawl underneath her. I want you to eat her pussy as if it's a gift from God himself." The woman's eyes widen as she glances at the scene behind me. This must be new to her. "You don't have to join in if you want to," I assure her, vaguely motioning around the room. "No one here will force you to do something you don't want to do. I'll make sure of it."

The woman glances back up towards me. "That's not it. I want to do this. I don't know how to get in there without someone stopping or getting hurt," She frets in an adorably innocent tone. I give her a reassuring smile and help her under my Goddess, placing her exactly where I want her. She reaches up and lays her hands on Lily's ribs, and starts licking and sucking on her clit with avidity. Lily's knees slide farther apart, dropping her lower onto the woman's mouth. Lily moans deeply.

I take Lily's hand and place it in between the woman's legs underneath her while using my shadows to hold her up. Leaning close to Lily's ear, I whisper, "Dinner is served, Goddess." I swear that I hear a primitive growl escape from her. It's as if some sort of switch was turned on, and she is lost to her needs. A dark blue haze emanates from her body. Forcing myself to maintain composure to this sudden change, my mind briefly loses focus on the sex.

Something is happening. Maybe this is what it's like when a succubus gets her fill. I'm drawn to her like a moth is to light as the smell of sweat and the distinct musk of sex drive my need higher. My hands ache with the demand to touch her skin and sink myself into her. My soul begs to hear her scream my name as she unravels for me.

I want to grab her and take her for myself. The world around us melts away and all I see is her. She's mine. My heart begins beating faster. I unzip my pants again, spit in my hand, and stroke myself feverishly. The sensation of heavenly pleasure tingles through me with each pass of my hand. My breath grows heavy and ragged, following the fall and rise of her chest.

I squeeze tighter as my dick gets harder in my hand and my pace quickens, shuddering each time it passes over the head collecting more pre-cum. Whatever reservation I had before is gone. I need this. Tension builds in my groin as the underside of my shaft buzzes with sensitivity with each pass. I need to give her this. Beads of sweat trickle down my face as I start thrusting into my firm grip. All for her. Everything for-

In unison, all five of us succumb to our desires, chasing the pleasure that has been building. Blue wisps float in the air, following an invisible path to her. Lily becomes relentless as the man that was in her mouth fills her throat with his cum. She swallows hard, licking her lips, before her ravenous gaze falls to the woman's dripping pussy underneath her.

Without reservation, she drops herself onto the woman and laps up the pleasure that drips from her pussy. Lily twirls her tongue around the woman's clit, reviving the memory of her orgasm and drawing out another. The woman starts to squirm wildly. Lily lets the blonde beauty clamp her legs onto the sides of her head and starts grinding her own hips on the woman's face. She wraps her arm around the woman's leg, thrusting her fingers deep inside. The woman tosses her head

back as another orgasm is pulled out of her body. Her hips buck and grind at Lily.

Without stopping, Lily lifts her face and places her arms between the woman's legs, spreading them apart. She inserts two more fingers into her glistening entrance and massages her clit with her thumb. As the woman writhes in pleasure, more wisps of blue light float towards Lily.

I make one final swipe across my dick clearing it of any remaining cum before fixing my pants to my waist. "Is my Goddess satisfied with her offering?" I ask, my voice raspier than usual in the aftermath of our festivities. Lily doesn't answer at first. Seemingly satisfied with her feast, Lily slowly pulls her thoroughly coated hand out, bringing it to her face. One by one, she sucks the thick creamy pleasure off her fingers, groaning at the taste.

Lily seductively drags her tongue across her palm cleaning up every last drop before making her way to the edge of the bed. The woman doesn't move as Lily climbs off of her, panting heavily, mumbling something along the lines of gratitude. As Lily's feet touch the ground, my body trembles. "More." she growls.

24

Lily

I don't want to stop. I need more. I want to eat my fill and then some. Living on scraps has taken a toll on me and that sensation is fading away. I was starving. Sam has been watching me closely this whole time, even as I suck the last of the woman's sweet nectar from my fingers. I carefully lick in between each one, making sure to get every last drop. It's sweet and thick. As I stand, I feel the cum that was dumped into me spill out, coating my inner thighs.

I walk out of the room to look for a bathroom; I want to clean myself off a little. The sweat on my body dried quickly, making my skin stick to itself. I make no attempt to grab my clothes. I won't be putting them back on anytime soon. Walking through this banquet makes my stomach growl. More.

I begin to lose myself again to the cracking sound of impact on skin and lamentations of people in all directions as they plead for their needs to be fulfilled. My legs are wobbly and weak. Each step I take is an effort. It's as if I've had one too many drinks and can't find solid ground.

Despite the luxury of the rest of the building, the restroom was clearly designed for easy cleanup and to serve its intended purpose. The only difference it has compared to any other public bathroom is a small bench and a shelf containing an array of feminine products, folded white towels, mouthwash, and some baby wipes.

I take a few baby wipes to clean between my legs. A toilet flushes and a woman steps out of the stall. She looks at me through the long mirror covering the wall above the sinks. "You look like you're having a great time. I haven't seen you here before."

I toss the baby wipe and grab another. "No, this is my first time here. I've been to sex clubs before, but nothing like this." The woman turns on the water and starts to wash her hands.

"Are you here to eat or be eaten?" I stop cleaning myself mid-wipe and look at her confused through the mirror. "Oh, you didn't know? Forget what I said." the woman says in an abrupt high pitch tone.

I put my leg down and toss the wipe in the trash. "Don't you mean Dom or Sub?" I've been to plenty of den parties and sex clubs. The casualness of the conversation is right on par, but the language she uses to describe your role is not. Maybe it's something new.

She turns the water off and grabs a hand towel. "No, I said what I mean. I'm here to eat," she replies, one eyebrow lifting in silent appraisal as she gazes unabashedly at my nakedness. "By the looks of you, I would say the same. You're practically glowing." She pats her hands dry and tosses the rag into the basket nearby.

"I'm sorry, but I really don't know what you mean by that," I say almost cautiously even as I find myself taking a step closer to her, the need to know almost a gravitational force pulling me toward this stranger. This is not the time to start talking about what I am. I need her to spell this out for me.

She grabs a small paper cup and fills it with mouthwash. She gestures nonchalantly toward me with her other hand before remarking, "You're a Succubus, right? Consuming the lust and desire of men and women." My jaw drops slightly as I take a cautionary step back. How does she know? Are there more of us? There is something about her that feels familiar. "Wait a second. I know you!" she exclaims in sudden realization. "Did Samael not tell you what this place was before he brought you here? I'm fairly certain I saw you walking in together. I just didn't realize that you would heal so quickly!" She tosses the liquid in her mouth and swishes it about.

My body goes stiff. I'm not jealous, but I sure as fuck want to know how this woman knows Sam. "Who are you, and how do you know us?" I snap, masking the fear settling within me. She spits the green liquid into the sink and wipes her face.

"I'm sorry, where are my manners?" She reaches her hand out towards me. "Asmodeus, she/they. I own this place. Sam called me to come help you after you got hurt. It makes sense that you don't recognize me. You were looking rough. I'm like you, sort of." My head spins at her confession. There are more like me. Others. I'm not alone. How does Sam know what I am?

"I don't understand. How do you know what I am?" I take a seat on the bench. My chest feels tight. What the fuck is going on here. I need to find Sam. How can she tell that I'm a succubus? Does that mean Sam is one too?

Asmodeus walks over to me and kneels to meet my eyes, her own expression calm and reassuring. "Talk to me, Lily. You don't know me well, but I'm a fantastic listener. Let me help."

My body starts trembling. I don't know what I am feeling right now. Deceived? Relief? Overwhelmed? Grateful? There are too many emotions at once.

My face feels tight as I try to hold back the tears. "I don't understand. I thought I was alone. I thought I was the only one who was like this. Now you're here telling me that there are others and that Sam knew. How did he know? Is he like this?" It all makes more sense. The reason he doesn't want to touch me. He must be like me and didn't want to hurt me the same way I was afraid to hurt him.

"I can't tell you about Sam, doll," Asmodeus replies almost regretfully. "That's not my place. He needs to talk about that with you. What I can tell you is that man out there has moved mountains to get you *everything* you needed to survive and heal. He only knew about me and this place once our mutual friend connected us. I will tell you the same thing I told him. You are not alone. You never were and never will be," her voice, strong and assuring.

Asmodeus takes a deep breath before she continues, "There are so many of us out there. I make it my life's mission to help demons like us. There are places like this across the country with people like me who have the same mission. Demons like us attract the worst kind of people, and we need each other to hold on to when the world works against us." I can see in her eyes how deep those wounds go.

Somehow, I know everything Asmodeus says is true. She knows exactly what I've gone through. I would bet any amount of money they have been through the worst, too. "Whatever negative thoughts or feelings you have for that amazing hunk of a man, get rid of it. The type of admiration that Sam has for you is rare," she advises before shooting me a wry grin. "Now we can sit here in our feelings, wishing for it all to be different, or we can put on our big girl panties and eat your heart out." Asmodeus helps stand me up. Somehow, I feel better despite hardly having a conversation. "You look skinny, and I know for a damn fucking fact that you're still hungry."

I nod my head in acknowledgment, shaking off the feelings of doubt. "Thank you. Just one last question." Asmodeus's face softens. "What do you mean you're sort of like me?"

She chuckles with a broad smile. "I was assigned male at birth. Male sex demons are called incubi. Females are called succubi. Why we are called something different based on our gender at birth is beyond me. Now stiffen your bottom lip, get out there, and do your stuff. We have a long night ahead of us, and based on how you smell right now, you want someone tall, tan, and handsome."

Asmodeus helps me clean up and get myself what she calls "sexified." I have so many questions for her. I could spend the rest of the night just talking. She insists that we meet up another day. I guess the sexual tension is palpable and needs to come to an end. Asmodeus playfully smacks my ass on her way out of the bathroom. I already feel that we are going to become best friends. I have so much to learn; now I know we have a community. I'm not alone, and I have never been.

I spot Sam staring out into the crowd when I leave the bathroom. He brings a glass filled with amber liquid to his mouth. The shadows of people walking past him add depth to his mask. As much as I want to stay here, we can always come back. I walk up to him and wrap my arms around his waist. Sam's face softens when he looks down at me and smiles. Wrapping his arm around me, he kisses the top of my head. "Let's go home." I encourage, resting my head on his chest.

Sam gives me a final squeeze then goes to locate my dress. When he returns, Sam helps me back into it, making sure I'm steady through my fatigue. Once we get into the car, I realize I feel like a new woman. Maybe I've had it wrong the whole time. If everything Asmodeus said is true, then Sam will already know what I am. He probably knows more about me than I do. If he isn't afraid of sleeping with a sex demon, then why should I be?

The car ride is silent as I'm lost in my thoughts. This has been one of the best nights of my life. When we first got here and stepped into the playroom it felt as if I was aligning with my true self. The confidence that came over me felt amazing and knowing that Sam was okay with me doing who and what I want made it that much better.

Having him watch me while all those people were on me, eating my fill drove me to a new height of release. I felt so powerful and more in control than I ever had before. All of their desires fill me, satiating that hunger in a way I have never experienced.

Maybe it was because for the first time I was actually able to let go. Be myself and take everything I want without having to cater to someone else's needs. For the first time in a long time, I am satiated. There is no primal force deep within me begging for what little scraps I can find.

As we get back to the house, we waste no time taking another shower together. I was only able to clean up enough so there wasn't cum dripping out of me. The smell of sex and sweat coat our skin. This time, I'm washing Sam. He deserves the attention just as much as I do. Especially since all he did was watch me get fucked and completely organized a scene. "Why didn't you tell me?" I question meekly.

I feel Sam's body stiffen under the loofa. "What do you think I haven't told you?" his body and tone in conflict. I take my time scrubbing every part of him. I need to choose my words carefully.

"That you're like me," I probe casually, as if we have had this conversation a thousand times over. I love that even though he's strong and muscular, he isn't one of those guys with washboard abs. His body is thicker in all the right places. Not so much that anyone can consider Sam unhealthy, but just enough so it conveys that he can handle a woman my size and that I won't break him. It gives him a softness that proves he's real.

Sam turns around, stopping me from washing him up. His face is soft yet stern. "Who told you that I'm like you?" he demands with appraising eyes.

I go back to washing him. Sam doesn't protest. "I met Asmodeus at the club. She didn't tell me in so many words that you are like me; I kinda put the pieces together," I tell him genuinely, taking care to scrub around his neck..

Sam stops me from washing him again, this time taking the loofa out of my hand and dropping it on the tub floor. "Goddess, I need you to look at me." He holds both of my hands, and I feel him trembling. He shifts back and forth on his feet as if something is wrong. "I didn't know how to tell you this. Before this night gets too far, I need you to know who I really am."

This does not sound good. "Ookay?" Now I'm starting to feel nervous.

Sam takes a deep breath. "I am not like you. I'm not a succubus or an incubus. I'm not even a demon." I'm hanging onto every word. "I'm the Devil."

Reflexively, I start laughing hysterically. "The Devil? You mean to tell me that you, Samael, are the literal devil?" Sam doesn't move. His stoic disposition sombers me a little. "You're not joking, are you?"

"No. I'm not. I understand if that makes you uncomfortable, but I need you to know." Oh shit. He's actually serious. I don't feel uncomfortable. If anything, it's kinda hot.

I step out of the shower and dry off, making sure not to dry between my legs. "Well, if you're really the devil, let's see how devilish you can really be." I want Sam to feel how wet he makes me. How much my body pines for him. Instead of handing the towel to him, I drop it on the ground and walk out to the bedroom. I feel his eyes watching me as I reach the bed. I turn slowly, putting my curves on full display, before perching on the edge of the mattress and opening my legs. Sam pauses in the doorway, towel in hand. "Your Goddess demands that you worship her, just as you've promised." I demand huskily, pouring my need for him, and solely him, into every word.

His eyes darken, and that twisted, devilish grin I've come to love grows across his face. "As you wish." Sam drops the towel and stares at me, closing the distance between us with a few quick strides. His intoxicating arousal sends a pang of need through me. He kneels down at the base of the bed in front of me making my muscles tighten in anticipation.

Sam delicately grabs my legs and kisses them inch by erotic inch as he makes his way to my pussy. He pauses just before my slit. His warm breath drives my need higher. I feel myself clench as he brushes his lips across my skin. "I am not worthy," he whispers in reverence. Without mercy, Sam plunges his tongue between my folds, licking me from taint to clit. His moans vibrate against me, sending a thrill of pleasure through my body.

I lay back on the bed as his tongue skillfully swipes across my clit. My knees fall to the sides, giving him more space. My body relaxes. The only thing I focus on are the sensations he bestows upon me. He pushes his face into me more, dragging his tongue from my taint to my clit. I make no attempt to silence myself. I let the whimpers fall out of me. Sam reaches up across my body, grabbing a hold of my nipple, twirling it in his fingers, driving my pleasure to greater heights. When he slips his fingers into me, my inner walls seize and there is no holding back. A deep, primal moan follows my orgasm. "That's my good girl." he growls.

When he stands, I can see that he is ready. His sizable dick swollen, thick, and just as needy. "If it pleases my Goddess, I want to watch how you fall apart for me." I chuckle at the sight of him bowing, my need never wavering. Sam gets onto the bed and pulls me up to the head of it. "I need to hear you say it. Laughter doesn't mean yes," he says almost teasingly, his large hand holding my face gently.

My brain goes on the fritz catching a glimpse of a smoldering flame in his eyes. It's more intense than anyone I saw tonight. He rubs the tip of his cock up and down through my folds bringing me back to focus. I want him inside of me so badly. "Fuck me," I beg, arching my back slightly with each passing swipe.

He draws the tip down, teasing my entrance. "Thank you, Goddess," he whispers, his breath hot against my ear. There's no ignoring the throbbing need deep within my stomach as Sam slowly pushes inside my entrance. I close my eyes and the back of my head digs into the mattress as he stretches me out, filling me completely.

When he reaches the hilt of his cock he drops his body on top of me. "You feel so good wrapped around my cock." his words trembling just before his lips touch my nipple with tantalizing possessiveness. I may not be much of a missionary girl, but this feels right. Intimate. Sam slowly moves in and out of me, rolling his hips in a way that adds just enough pressure to my clit.

I place the tips of my toes on his calves, curling into the curve of his body. Each thrust feels deeper than the last at this angle. Another orgasm builds up and escapes with an explosion that causes my core to tighten. My nails dig into his back as I fall into its ecstasy.

Sam's hands lightly trace a path over my skin as he reaches my hands sending pleasant jolts through my body. His quivering, tentative touch has me writing beneath him, eager for more. It's flesh against flesh, man against woman, and his tormented groans are a heady invitation to finally let go.

The real world spins and careens on its axis, as the last breath of my defenses weaken to a love that flows like warm honey. He moves my hands on top of each other and pins them down, taking the free hand to gather me snugly against his body. Sam isn't merely filling a moment of physical desire, he may not know it, but I will allow him to tear my soul apart.

With a deep thrust I shatter into a million glowing stars and bury my face against his throat. Our sweaty bodies brush against each other in exquisite harmony with one another. As his grip tightens, I pull my head back away from his body and that devilish smile reappears. "Eyes on me, Goddess." he grunts before smothering my lips with demanding mastery.

25

Samael

Lily's enchanting brown eyes lock onto me. She feels so soft. It's as if I'm enveloped in liquid velvet. With her arms held above her and legs wrapped around me, I hold back the urge to go deeper. The warmth and wetness enveloping me as I pump in and out of her forces a raw passion to rise in me like the hottest fire, clouding my brain. My Goddess's orgasm is written all over her face as she moans with erotic pleasure.

The way she clenches her jaw when I grind into her again, chasing another, can't disguise her body's reaction. Her walls squeeze me from all sides, then open up as divine nectar seeps out. I let go of her hands and prop myself up slightly. Blue flames begin to reflect in her eyes as her breath comes out in long surrendering moans. It's as if a dormant sexuality of her body has been awakened and I am honored to be the one to set her free.

Lily wraps her arms around me and claws at my back. The sting of digging her nails into my skin only heightens the experience. I know she wants to close her eyes. She's doing such a good job watching me. Every time her breasts bounce, her nipples gently brush against my chest.

"Sam. Don't. Stop," she pants between thrusts. Fuck me. Famous last words. I won't, Goddess. I grab ahold of her neck and add the slightest of pressure.

"Cum for me," I urge and she erupts on command. Knowing that I have complete control over her body makes our vulnerability seem more pronounced. Her breath becomes ragged. The pressure that is built is almost too much. I slam myself into her. Her screams will forever be etched into my mind. The tingling of release makes me buckle. Trying to push every last inch of myself deeper and deeper as I cum and her body vibrates with liquid fire.

Slowly, I pull myself out and collapse next to her panting heavily. When our breaths settle, I reverently clutch Lily's body, never wanting to let go. She pushes her ass against me, wiggling it until it is tucked perfectly within my curves. "Stay," I whisper in her ear. She doesn't move or speak a word. I lift myself up. As I brush the hair away from her face, I find my Goddess fast asleep. I reach over and kiss her cheek, "Please, stay."

* * *

As I slowly open my eyes, I'm greeted by the soft glow of the morning sun filtering through the curtains. The light dances across the room as if the sun is whispering that it is time to wake up. Taking a deep, cleansing breath, the promise of possibilities fills my lungs. With a sigh, I stretch my limbs, reveling in the sensation of every muscle waking. The sheets cradle my body in a warm embrace. I roll to my side, reaching out for Lily.

Nothing but the chill of empty sheets finds my hands. Please. No. My eyes shoot open. Whatever morning haze I had disappears at the sight of where Lily slept, lying empty. No. No. No. I jump out of bed and run to the closet. She packed clothes. I know she did. The doors to the closet fly open, slamming against the wall. I search for them in every nook and cranny, pressure building in my chest with each passing second. Where are they? Please no. It was perfect. Everything was so perfect. How could she leave?

I run down the stairs, jumping over the last few, and frantically search every room for any evidence of Lily. Anything. Fuck. I'll take anything. Goddess. Please. Fuck. Fuck. Fuck. I make my way to the kitchen. Nothing. There's not even a cup in the sink. The bathroom. Maybe she's in the bathroom. With equal speed, I run back to the master bathroom. Skipping steps on my way up.

The bathroom door slams open. Empty. Dry. She isn't here. She isn't fucking here. My fist flies through the bathroom wall, creating a deep hole. The pain in my hand feels like nothing compared to my heart.

I find my way back to the edge of the bed and sit. That's it, then. A heaviness comes over me. She's gone. Numbness begins to replace panic. She left and she isn't coming back. My Goddess. My heart and soul. Vanished. I slide down onto the floor as my eyes fill with tears that threaten to escape.

I feel nothing.

Nothing and everything all at once.

Beep Beep Beep

Every ounce of my being wants to stay here. The floor is my sanctuary. If I leave, it solidifies that she isn't coming back.

Beep. Beep. Beep. Just stop. Please. *Beep. Beep. Beep.* I groan, getting up. I shut off the alarm. Might as well get ready and go to work. There's nothing left for me to do. I made a promise, and she made her choice. I can either be a man of my word or go against everything I've made my name for.

People know I won't make a deal and not follow through. After a quick shower, I put on a suit, swallow my emotions, and leave. I was ready for her to be here and to call off work. I even told Hal he could take the day off. Before I close the door, I stand on my stoop and wait a few more minutes on the off chance that she changes her mind and comes back to me. She doesn't.

The sound of the door locking behind me is the last nail in my coffin. I place the stone-hearted mask that has gotten me this far in life on as if it has never left me.

Every moment of the day is like a faint memory. I know I was there, but it feels like I am watching from the outside. I went to all of her favorite spots just in case she was there. There was no sign of her at the coffee shop. The day passes painfully slow. I don't have the energy to deal with Michael or the justice system. I decide to stop at Mr. M's shop after work. I know she would be there. If I could just see her one last time.

I sit in my car trying to decide if going into the shop is the right decision, waiting to see if I can spot her through the window or walk through the door. I need to make sure she is okay. That she got to where she wanted to go. Five or ten minutes pass and there's still no sign of her. I muster up the courage and step out of the car. I can do this. I can do this.

My heart hammers in my chest with each step I take closer to the bookshop. Tension builds as I reach for the brass handle.

I can do this. The door, once so light, feels weighted as I open it. The bells chime above, announcing my arrival. I can do this. "Samael! How marvelous it is to see you, my boy!"

The world speeds up, bringing me back to the present. I became aware of my surroundings once more. "It's good to see you too, Mr. M." Feigning a smile, I shake his hand.

"What can I help you with today? Looking for something new to get our Lily?" He asks in a chipper tone while reaching under the counter. "I just got a few books that I think she is going to enjoy." Mr. M grunts lightly pulling out a pile of books then going back for more. "Since she came back, I felt it was time to start expanding my collection to include more modern writing. I'm even considering expanding the shop." A determined glint shines brighter behind his eyes with each book he produces.

Pick up books? Lily? That doesn't make sense. Mr. M wouldn't ask that if she was here. Maybe he doesn't know. This isn't right. He must know… he's practically her father. "Is she not here?" I ask, my hackles rising with every word. Mr. M rises from behind the counter.

His brows furrow like an accordion as he fumbles with his glasses, finally taking them off and setting them down on the counter with a clatter. "No, why would Lily be here, son?" he asks in a stern voice only a father can muster.

The shop door creeks shut behind me, the momentary silence slamming into me like a punch to the gut. Lily should be here, curled up in her usual chair by the fireplace, book in hand or wondering about helping customers. My mind reels over our conversation and my promise to let her go after last night. Panic claws at my throat. "I woke up this morning, and she wasn't at the house. I had assumed she would be here."

The pieces just don't fit. This doesn't make any sense.

Mr. M reaches into his sweater vest pocket with measured deliberations, his fingers emerging a pristine white handkerchief. He picks up his glasses and begins cleaning them with a steady hand. "Did you have a fight this morning?" His tone is cold and calculating. "I may not be her biological father, but I will not take it lightly if you hurt her heart." Such a frail figure to be making veiled threats. If he were any other man I would show him the error of his ways. But Lily... the love shines in his glossy eyes with the same fierce protectiveness I feel for her. He loves her just as much as I do, if not more.

The defiance drains out of me and is replaced with a weary sigh, "No, we didn't fight. I woke up, and she wasn't there." Wait, this morning? His words explode through my mind making my blood run cold. "What happened this morning?" I blurt out, a knot of tension in my jaw growing like a vice. Every fiber of my being screams danger. I don't care how, I have to figure out what is going on.

"Lily called me early this morning. She was on her way to the coffee shop and told me that she decided she wasn't going to need to stay here. I was elated that you and Lily hit it off so well that you decided to go steady. I didn't like her last fella as much as I do you. Besides, you've taken good care of my Lily after the house fire. It's a shame that place burned down." Go steady? Not stay here.

My fingers fumble as I pull out my phone, the screen flashing in the dim light. I go to my contact favorites and tap her name, praying for an answer. The first ring echoes through me, then the second, each one a hammer to my already racing heart. My stomach clenches at the cheery tone of her voicemail. This isn't like her. I hang up and try again. She must be busy or maybe she just doesn't want to talk to me, I reassure myself. But a nagging voice in the back of my mind whispers a different story.

The room seems to shrink with the walls closing in on me. A finally booming surge of panic rushes through me. "Thank you, Mr. M. I have to go. I'll be back later." I mutter quickly, rushing to the door. Heart hammering in my chest, I grip the handle and fling the door open while calling Levi. Fucker. Pick up faster.

My common sense takes a backseat to raw panic. Without a second thought, I bolt across the street, weaving between startled pedestrians and the screech of tires muted against the ringing of my phone. "Hey boss man, what's happening?" Levi's relaxed voice infuriates me. I swear he's more of a man-child than Hal.

With a desperate yank, I fling my car door open and practically throw myself into the driver's seat. "Levi, I need you to track Lily's cell phone and tell me where it is. I think it might be dead or shut off or fucking something." There is no hiding the fear in my voice. The engine roars to life and I slam it into reverse, squealing my tires as I race into traffic.

"You got it. Just give me a second." I can hear his fingers smashing on the buttons of his keyboard. "Alright, it looks like her last known location is at your house. Are you two playing some sort of kinky hide-and-seek? I fucking love that shit." he chuckles.

The engine releases a guttural roar as I slam the gas pedal to the floor board. "Damn it Levi! Not now! Can you tell me if she even left the house today?" The needle of my speedometer gradually rises as I weave through the maze of cars on the way to my house. Horns blare at my reckless driving, though they are nothing more than a blur in my peripheral vision.

"Doesn't look like it, boss. From what I'm seeing here, she's been at your house since around two this morning." She wasn't there. I searched that whole fucking house and there was no sign of her. The clothes were even gone.

My knuckles whiten as I grip the steering wheel, the leather becoming slick with the sweat from my palms. "Listen, this is the one and only time I'm going to give you this permission. Tap into my door camera and view the movement history. I swear to God Almighty himself, if you don't sign the fuck off after thi-" My tires scream as the car drifts around the corner pushing me with it. A trail of smoke billows behind me as I take the next corner just as fast.

"You'll kill me. I know the drill." His fingers must be moving faster than earlier. I dodge the last few cars in my way. Almost there. "Time clock shows her leaving the house at 7:05 and turning right off the porch. Then I see you leaving at 9:14." That means she must have left half an hour before I woke up.

"This is really important. Was Lily carrying anything when she left," I ask, a distant part of myself surprised by the desperate thread of hope woven into my voice. If she didn't take her clothes, that means what Mr. M said is true. She really didn't leave me. There is no reason for him to lie to me. Even if he did, I would be able to tell. But that also means that I'm right and there is something horrifyingly wrong.

"Negative on that one, boss. Unless you count a purse, but that's more of an accessory, or so I've been told." Pull up to the house and park. There's no time for pleasantries. I hang up the phone and run into the house. My heart is pounding in my ears.

"Lily!" No response. I run through the house at lightning

speed. Checking every room for her one by one. She's not here. The upstairs is empty as well. "Lily!" Not even a chuckle. She wouldn't play a fucked up game like this. Taking a minute to observe every corner of the room, even if I can find her phone. I walk in circles. Looking under the bed, on the floor, the dresser, the closet. Where the fuck is it? That's when I see it. A small piece of paper peeking out from under her pillow.

Sam,

Didn't want to wake you. Went to get tea. Be back soon.
-Your Goddess

26

Lily

Drip
Drip
Drip

Fuck, my head hurts. I have to rub my eyes a few times before they get with the picture and gain focus. Even with that, everything is still dark and blurry. The thick air smells like a strange mix of dampness and smoke, making it difficult to take an easy breath. Where the hell am I? Rubbing my eyes again clears up more of the haze. "Hello?" That hurts. My throat and mouth feel like I've swallowed sandpaper and glass.

I push myself off the dirt-covered floor. Ew. It feels thick and goopy. Please don't be poop. That would be so gross. I wipe my hands off on my shirt. "Hellooo." My footsteps echo against the water-logged floor. Cautiously, I try to navigate through the murky space. How the hell did I get here? The last thing I remember is leaving the house to get tea for Sam and me.

Water drips steadily from above. There's a window, at least. Leave it to me to trip and fall into a pit of despair. The little light there is beams in just enough that I can make out most of this place. The walls are charred and blackened. I can almost make out what appears to be broken pipes above me. I gotta get out of this place. I search my pockets for my phone. Awesome, I lost that too. Now, I can't even call for help or use the flashlight.

I search the ceiling more for the spot that I must have fallen through. This doesn't make any sense. How did I get in here if there isn't a hole? I take a hesitant step forward. My heart starts to race in my chest. This isn't right. Every sound down here becomes so loud. What the fuck is going on? It's like my body knows something I don't, putting me in overdrive. My next step is halted.

No, no, no, no, no, no. "Help!" I'm chained. "Help!" I can't get out. "Someone help! I'm down here!" I take both of my hands and grab onto the rubber-coated chain. Panic quickly takes over. I yank at the chain praying for my freedom. Every wave of the chain comes to a swift halt. My shoulders pop as I dig my heels into the wet ground, pulling against it. "Let me out of here!" I shriek, my desperation forced through gritted teeth. I lose my footing and fall right on my ass.

Mud cakes under my fingerI scrape them across the ground picking the chain back up. It makes little noise as I move around the room carrying it. I need to figure out if I can even reach anything. Every time the chain stops at its full length, it feels like another stone drops in my stomach. My chest tightens with panic. "Control yourself Lily. You can't lose your shit now." My own words do little to reassure me. There is maybe fifteen, no twenty feet, of room for me to move on this stupid chain. Dammit my spatial awareness is absolute crap. That has to be why I'm such a klutz.

Fuck this. I drop the chain and work on my ankle which is wrapped in some kind of thick leather cuff with a thick ring and a heavy duty padlock. My hands tremble from fear-fueled adrenaline and pain as I mess around with it. This is some horror movie-type shit, and I'm not about it. Damn it. I need a key. I swear to all things good in this world, there'd better not be any creepy ass doll popping up asking me to play a game. I will die down here.

I need to find a rock or something sharp enough to cut this. I get up from the ground again and start looking. Charred wood. That's not going to work. Uhhhh. Oh, what about this! I pick up a stone or maybe a piece of chipped concrete. It's better than nothing. Sitting back in the mud, I position the lock as flat as possible. Useless movie knowledge; don't fail me now! Drawing the stone-like thing high above me, I swing it down onto the lock with all my force. If I can hit this hard enough, I can break it and get the fuck out of here.

I raise my arm up and start hammering at the lock again. Come on. Give. Up. You. Stupid. Piece. Of. Metal. My chest burns for fresh air. This isn't working. Fuck you movies. You could have saved my life right about now. I drop the stone and lay back on the cold, wet floor in starfish depression. I guess I'll just wait it out then. There isn't any other way out of here, seeing as how I'm chained to the fucking wall. "Hello, can anyone hear me?" The words fall out with none other than defeat laced throughout my tone.

Drip, Drip, Drip. At this point, I might as well wait for whoever came up with this brilliant plan to come back. Who knows how long that will even take. If it was me, I would wait until it got dark. That way, no one would notice where I was going. If I've learned anything from all of those criminal documentaries, this person has a huge set of balls. It was literally broad daylight. Although, generally, those people in the documentaries die. So, I should probably start getting comfortable with that idea. "Hello! Echo! Is anyone out there who isn't trying to kill me? Follow the sound of my voice!"

Maybe they are like a professional serial killer. That would be interesting. Or what if it's some sort of crazy stalker who has watched one too many of my videos. Really should have thought twice about making the kidnapping one. Clearly hindsight is 20/20 there. Especially if this is the outcome.

Do they not understand that it's just content to make money? Then again, that's assuming there is someone out there who is obsessed with me like that. Wow, even in the worst scenario possible, my head is inflating. Quite an inflated ego you got there, Lily. Dial it back a bit, babe. You're not that famous.

Then again, no one can forget about what happened to Alexandria Randolph. That chick had it all. The beauty, the fame, the subscribers, the butt load of money. Nobody realized she was even missing until they found her body at the bottom of a lake. That's why I never scheduled any of my posts. Her channel went on for about 3 weeks. The news went wild. They eventually ended up figuring out that one of her fans became so desperate for her attention that he snuck into her house and played with her organs. The man literally cut her open and played around with her entrails.

A shiver rolls up my spine. Okay, maybe I don't want to be that famous. "Hello! Can anyone hear me? Anyone whatsoever!"

"Hello?" Holy shit. I sit up and search for the person behind the voice. "Oh my God. Are you okay? How did you get in there?" A shadowed face peeks in through the window.

I get as close to the window as possible. "Please help me. Get me the fuck out of here."

His head moves back and forth. My savior! "Listen, I need you to wait there. It doesn't look safe for me to go inside. This place is basically burnt to a crisp. I'm going to call for help."

"There's no time!" I scream. Realizing that blind panic may not actually help persuade my would be rescuer, I take a deep breath and try again, practically shaking with the effort to speak more calmly. "I realize this isn't the ideal situation, but I'm chained to the wall. Someone abducted me, and I woke up," I motion to all around me. "Wherever this is. I need you to get me out before they come back. I don't know how long we have left, and if we are being honest with each other, I'm freaking out." His feet shuffle across the gravel as he stands up. "No, please! Don't leave me down here!"

"Just hang on. I'll be right there." When he walks away, I can only stand here and listen. *Creeeeek* "I'm coming in now. What's your name?" I grab the rock I used to try to break myself out of here and slam it off the pipes above my head. The sound reverberates through the room.

I can hear that his footsteps are slow and careful. I can hear the slow creaking above get closer to where I'm banging. "Lily. Who do I, very literally, owe my life to?" The sound of his footsteps feels like an angelic chorus overhead.

My pulse quickens as I search frantically for the exit in hopes that I can give him an idea of where I am. "Lily? Is that really you? It's your neighbor, Michael LaBorn." His footsteps walk away from where I was banging. My neighbor? That would mean… I hear him pause. "Hey man, I don't know what the big idea is." I didn't even hear another set of footsteps. Has there been someone listening to me down here the entire time?

"You need to back off. I'm warning you! I don't care if you're-"
Thump.

Dust falls from overhead.

Stomp

Stomp

Stomp

Reeeeeeeeeek

Light filters in from an opening. A door. There's a way out. I think it might be close enough for me to get to. My breath quivers. My heartbeat races in my ears. Shit. I think Mike is dead. Whoever that is must have killed him. A small object comes in through the opening, then the hatch is slammed shut. Footsteps boom overhead and then fade away.

I'm not sure how long I stay frozen in place just listening. Waiting for any sign of movement from above. A warm, wet drop hits my forehead. I wipe it off, putting my hand closer to the light to see what it is. Blood. He's dead. My savior is dead, and I'm alone with a murderer.

27

Samael

The air inside St. Augustine's is thick, just the same as it always has been. The mix of stale smoke, cheap booze, and the faint scent of piss doesn't faze me like it used to. On any other day, I would be drawn into nostalgia. However, today, St. Augustine fuels my determination that much more. The dim flickering neon lights barely illuminate the worn-out stools. The bartender, August, watches carefully as I make my way to the Ferryman's table. He knows. August has seen this scene play out one too many times.

All eyes are on me when I reach the top of the short staircase and take my rightful place. I'm not above calling in my favors. I need everyone on this. I could call my team and do what needs to be done, but that won't help me find Lily faster. Not when there are treaties to consider. Lines have been drawn, and if I'm not careful, I can start a war far earlier than planned.

Hal is the first to arrive. He silently takes his place next to me. As my right-hand man, he already knows the drill. August walks up to us with a glass in hand. "You've got the same look on your face that your father had when business was booming."

He sets my usual on the table. "The Ferryman always collects his tolls. Don't forget it."

One by one, enemies and colleagues filter in and take their place around the table. Manny, Levi, and Dis sit around me. I don't generally like to call Dis into these matters. However, his qualifications outweigh my indifference. He will never say exactly what he did. He can only say that he's served multiple tours in Iraq and Afghanistan. I can appreciate his ability to keep his mouth shut. The military turned mercenary.

It's no coincidence that Dis is in this line of work solely based on his appearance. Dis is always wearing dark blue jeans, a white V-neck t-shirt, black boots, and a black leather jacket. A large scar runs diagonally across his face and into his non-existent hairline. His dead brown eyes rarely convey any expression and frequently exhibit his patented thousand yard stare. There aren't many things that can make a man embody that much wrath. Whatever his reason, I'm confident that his rage is justified.

Michael and his team filter in a little later. August brings each of our respective men drinks, setting them carefully on the table without a single word or glance in anyone's direction. The tension from the partitioners, which seem like permanent fixtures at this point, can be cut with a knife. "What are we all here for, Samael?" demands Michael suddenly, impatience stamped onto every feature of his stupidly perfect face. "I had to call a recess on a murder trial to be here. It better be worth my time." Michael is always the first to speak and the last to take initiative.

A irate growl escapes Dis. I can tell he does not want to be here. Dis only recently came back from Miramar, the Naval Consolidated Brig, to negotiate a deal on my behalf.

I sit myself upright, squaring my shoulders out. "Lily is missing." Hal gasps behind me at my announcement. I can hear him shifting in his chair, discomfort emanating from him.

"You called this meeting because your girlfriend left you?" Michael sneers.

Levi slams his hands on the table. "She didn't leave. She was abducted, you fucking ass hat! Where is she?" I raise my hand to Levi, and he sits back down.

"Bold of you to assume that I would abduct a woman, let alone his woman. Do I look like an idiot? We are in peacetime, and I intend to keep it that way until one of you epically screws up." Michael's men are more tame than my own. He employs mindless, honest men who follow orders blindly.

I, however, do not. My men are killers, crooks, con artists, the most dangerous individuals society has to offer. I didn't employ them because they can follow orders. I employed them because they aren't afraid to get their hands dirty. Each of them has earned the opportunity to work with me because they know how to do the jobs that I need and have a similar level of morality. I don't care how they do it, but there is zero tolerance for violence against children or innocent women. "I called you here to see if you know anything about her whereabouts and to request your assistance in finding her. I do not have the time or patience to go to war with you today, brother."

Michaels's jaw tenses. I'll play the family card. He owes me for everything he has right now and knows it far too well. "What's in it for me if I help you?"

"If you or any member of your team find Lily and return her to me, you can consider your debt paid in full." Manny leans in. He knows me well enough to understand the gravity of my words. I've held onto Michael's debts for a long time. He's tried to pay it up, but nothing was worth more than the defeated look on his face when I refuse his offer. Then there is the added debt he has recently accumulated.

Michael's body grows tense. He should know well enough what it is that I am dealing with. With his childhood crush, Joan, being saved thanks to me, this is also a 'wash your back and you wash mine' agreement. Cornering him and exposing the fact that he made a deal with the devil to his team is the icing on the cake. "And if we don't?" Michael sneers. Checkmate.

I take a sip of the tart drink August made me. Having Michael search for Lily means that this city will be flipped upside down. Every law enforcement officer will be out there scouring the streets. "Fail to do so, and your debts remain unpaid." He wants this too much to not help me. "As an additional benefit, I'll even give you my blessing to send your teams into my territory for the search. Granted, this will last only until Lily is found. You will be contacted if we locate and rescue Lily first. Once that happens, your teams will have thirty minutes to get out of my territory. Anyone of them found after that will be in violation of our peace agreement and will be dealt with accordingly."

Michael's nose wrinkles as a disparagement forms across his face. He doesn't say a word. Take the deal. This is your only shot at getting out of my debt. He leans back into his chair and loosens his tie. We both know this is worth it. Trusting that he will make this a quick search and rescue is the leap of faith I'm willing to take. He can easily drag his feet, though that would mean he has fallen further than he is willing to admit.

Michael reaches his hand out to me. "You have yourself an

agreement. I'll find your girl, and we will all be paid up." I reach out and squeeze his hand with my full strength.

Locking eyes with Michael, I let the aura of my powers emanate from my side of the room. I feel the darkness growing behind me as my team releases theirs as well, showing that they are with me in whatever my decision is. "Fuck me over and you'll regret being born."

"My only regret is that you were born, brother." As we both stand, our constituents follow. The chairs are left open as Michael and his team leave the Ferryman's table. Their regimented steps vibrate the floor as they file out of St. Augustine's. Just before he leaves, Michael pulls out his phone and brings it to his ear. "Gabriel, it's me. We have work to do. Top priority." The door closes behind him.

Now that the meeting is over, my team continues to stand, waiting for their orders. "Levi, you're on surveillance. I want you to tap into every channel you can and watch them. If they find her first, I need to know. Start scanning public surveillance systems and see if you can get a lead on where Lily went and who is behind this." Levi nods and runs out of the bar.

"Manny, I need you to get you to get feet on the ground. I want as many people as you can spare." Manny stands from his chair and buttons his jacket up.

"Is there any chance that *she* is behind this?" he spat, retribution hardening his features. Thin trails of smoke leave his nostrils. Manny is desperate to get his hands on Ali. He will be properly motivated if he thinks she is behind Lily's abduction. Besides, I need him to be pissed off. He's more efficient that way.

"Don't think it isn't on my list. Lily disappeared too fast and clean for it not to be possible. With the appearance of Cain, we can only assume that Ali isn't far behind. She is coming back to town for a reason; the only question is, what does Lily have to do with it?" Manny leaves his chair open and walks out the door.

Dis stands from his chair. "I'll take over, looking in angel territory for any sign of her. If she is over there, I will find her." His gravelly voice has a deathly calmness to it. Dis grips my shoulder tightly. Without any further instruction, he leaves.

"What do you want me to do?" Hal gives me a sorrowful glance.

"I want you to go back to my house and wait there. If there is any possibility that Lily escapes on her own and goes back to the house, I need someone who she is familiar with and trusts to be the first face she sees." Hal's brows pinch together and his fists clench.

"You want me to sit around on my ass while everyone is out there searching for Lily?!" he blurts, his face redding with outrage. "Over these last few weeks, Lily and I have grown close. I know almost as much about her as you do! She may be your lover, but she is my friend." His anger is understandable. I can't even be mad at him. He has grown close to Lily and has been with her every second I was gone.

I place my hands on his shoulders. "I know that. Your friendship with both of us is the reason I can trust you, and only you, to do this. I trust you with my life, Hal. I also trust that if Lily shows up at that house, you will protect her till your last breath. So yes, I need you to be at the house and wait for her. If it is who I think is behind Lily's abduction, then there is a high possibility I won't be coming back alive." I reach behind me and grab my cursed pistol. Hal's face pales at its sight.

"You're not going to use that thing are you?" Hal whispers. I grab his hand and put the pistol in his palm. He slowly wraps his fingers around it.

I raise my head slowly to take a moment for a silent goodbye. My right hand man, my best friend, my family. Hal is everything a man would want in another as a friend. Pride swells inside my chest. "No, you are. Keep it safe, use it if you must." My throat tightens at every word. "It's been a privilege to know you, and an honor to be called friend."

Hal lunges forward, wrapping his arms around me in a hug. I hold onto him tight. "The honor has been all mine, Sammy," he says shakily.

28

Lily

It's getting harder to see. The little bit of light that I was getting from the sun filtering through the window has started to fade away. The room is now filled with a coppery tang of blood mingling with the damp mustiness of the basement. Since Michael LaBorn tried to rescue me, I haven't heard any footsteps, let alone any noise, coming from upstairs.

I can't figure it out. How did I end up close to my old neighbor? As far as I can remember, there aren't any abandoned homes nearby, and my house was the only one that was caught in a fire. This can't be my house. We didn't have a basement, or at least there was no access for us.

So far, all of my attempts at freedom have been futile. The chain won't budge. The lock won't smash. I can't get the leather around my ankle to loosen or rip. I have entirely run out of ideas. I probably should have spent more time dedicated to visiting escape rooms. If I escape here alive, that's going to be a weekly date night for Sam and me.

Then again, there is that thing that was tossed down here.

The chain is beginning to feel heavy on my leg. Let's also add going to the gym to my list of things to do after I escape. It's been on me all day at this point. The skin under and around it is so itchy. Making it a point to walk around the puddle of blood and mud, I make it close to where I think that thing fell. My hands become thick with soil as I pat around for it.

"Where the hell is it?" The more I search, the more I can feel my throat closing. I want this to be over. I want to go home. I want to be back with Sam. I start grabbing at whatever I can. Throwing rocks, pieces of splintered wood, and anything else nearby. My frustration boils over, forcing me to let out a guttural scream.

As I start to calm down, I sit on the floor, curling my knees to my chest. I wrap myself into a ball and just let it out. Tears stream down my face and the saliva in my mouth grows thick. This is what I'm reduced to. Helplessly hoping that some stupid fucking rando item that got tossed down here with me will be my ticket out of this nightmare.

Darkness settles in the room. My only companions are the sounds of crickets and dogs barking in the distance. The night air finds its way into the room, chilling me to the bone. This would be a beautiful night under any other circumstance. I love fall. Everything about it. Sam made it better.

We could be getting ready for Halloween. It's just around the corner. I could have decorated the house, and we would pass out candy to all of the trick-or-treaters in their cute little costumes. Go to the haunted houses. Maybe I would have been able to convince him to go apple picking with me. The tingling in my hands and feet become more pronounced. The chill makes them feel swollen and desperate for heat.

I tuck my hands under my arms in an attempt to warm them.

Laying here on the cold, hard ground forces my body to shiver against the chill of the settling night. Each breath I take is like a puff of mist in the air. The ground is unforgiving, pressing my bones every time I try to shift.

Exhaustion slowly creeps in as I focus on the sound of my heartbeat. The steady rhythm, like my personal melody, is enjoying every thump as if it's my last. The biting cold starts to numb my senses other than the chattering of my teeth.

My blinking becomes obviously slower with each passing moment. I know I should stay awake, but sleep sounds so good right now. Just as the darkness threatens to consume me, a faint golden pulse of light catches my attention on the floor.

It takes more energy than I want to exert to move through the chilling embrace of the night towards it. The tiny light begins to pulse brighter as I get close. Mesmerized, I reach out, touching the light. My stiff fingers wrap around it, dragging dirt and the light back to me. The warmth radiating from it sends a painful and relieving sensation to my hand. I clutch onto the luminous object, wishing I could absorb as much heat as possible. The icy chill that had settled deep in my bones begins melting away as waves of heat travel through me. With each passing moment, the numbness that had threatened me fades.

I cautiously open my hand to reveal what can conjure heat and light. My fingers tremble, not from the cold but from the fear that the promise of warmth will disappear. Swiping away the mud reveals a pendant slightly smaller than the palm of my hand. It grows brighter the more I look at it. Though somehow, its golden illumination doesn't hurt or strain my eyes.

Elegant curves and sharp angles sit at the center of a golden circle outline, seeming attached by three crosses. At what I can only assume is the top, a thin, leathery cord hangs. I've seen this before. Tracing my fingers along its smooth pattern, I scour my memory for its likeness. "Where do I know you from?"

Images buried in my memory come forth like a flash, playing like a movie. I see myself sitting in my chair at the bookshop. Mr. M standing next to me. Another flash. I'm looking into the book, and he points out the symbol in the top corner. Another flash. I'm with my mother. I can feel the burning sensation behind my eyes.

She rips a necklace out of my hands. Mom. My mom. Flash. I'm sitting in a car. My mother takes the necklace. Her voice echoes: "I'm doing this to protect you. So you can have a normal life." I don't remember any of this. How is this happening? She leaves the car. I watch through the window as she walks into a building. Tears stream down my face. With a final flash, I'm pulled back into the dreadful reality in which I exist.

My breathing is bordering on panting, the rapid pace tightening my chest. This. I hold the pendant up by its cord in front of my face. This is mine.

Thump. Thump. Thump. Shit. Pulling the cord over my head, I stuff the pendant down my shirt. Still too bright. I move it over and put it behind my padded bra. Thankfully, that works. The footsteps keep a steady pace. They walk all around the floor above me. Terror seeps into my core. There's nowhere to hide. The overhead hatch opens. "You're awake. Good," a feminine voice calls down. My body tenses at the thought that this is the person who abducted and trapped me.

I have fawned my entire life. I have been beaten bloody,

abducted, hospitalized, ostracized, raped, bones broken, manipulated, insulted, and controlled; my life has been a horror story. Not anymore. If I can stand up to Adam, I can fight this nasty piece of work. "Yeah, now why don't you come down here and let me out."

In a blink, the person disappears, then reappears right in front of me. How the fuck? "With the paycheck I'm about to receive for bringing you here?" She laughs maniacally. "I don't think so." A price tag?

"Tell me. How much is my life worth?" Standing, I casually try to brush the majority of the caked-on mud and dirt off my body.

"Enough for me to keep you alive." The shadow disappears. "I'm looking for something. A book." Her voice purrs from behind me. I know it's dark, but there is no reason I shouldn't be able to catch a glimpse of her moving around me.

I flip around trying to follow this psycho woman's movements. "Then go to a library." What the fuck? She was just here.

"This isn't just any book. It's an incredibly old book. You see, this particular book was stolen out of my archives many years ago. I've been trying to locate it for some time now. Let's just say it's a family heirloom." Her voice echoes from the far corner of the room. I follow it, straining my eyes trying to see clearly through the veil of shadows.

"Why the hell do you think I would know anything about a stolen book?" I may be a lot of things, but I am far from being a thief. I grab hold of the chain to take some of the weight off my ankle as I walk closer to the direction her voice came from.

"I've been watching you closely. Last night at the club, you proved that you not only saw it but also read from it."

I've read so many books. Now, this woman wants me to remember which one she's referring to? "Explain that one, brainiac."

"There isn't a single succubus alive with your amount of power. I watched you take and take and take. You consumed the soul of the devil himself. Did you really think that was normal for your kind?" she questions, raising an eyebrow. Normal? My entire life has been anything but normal. I thought this was just me for the longest time. It's not like I've had much to compare myself to, seeing I just found out there were more like me.

"I don't know what you're talking about," I declare flatly, even as realization begins to tingle through my bones. That would mean the singing book from Mr. M is the one she is talking about. I feel my heart begin to race deep within my chest. There is no way I can tell her that. If she can do all of this to me, she will kill Mr. M. I won't let that happen.

"Ah, so you do know the book I am talking about," she croons with more than a subtle hint of triumph. "I can hear it. Your heart is racing. I'm not in the mood to play around with you. I have more pressing matters to deal with. I'll let him handle it." Her dark chuckle sends a chill through me. I hear the hatch open and close again. If none of what I can do is normal...then what am I?

An unnatural silence stretches, broken only by the frantic beating of my own heart. Glowing green orbs, like malevolent fireflies, pierce through the dark oppressive shadows that blanket the room. A wave of nausea washes over me, threatening to release pure bile all over the floor.

The eyes lock onto me with a predatory glint, hitching my

breath in my throat. Every fiber of my being screams to run, but there is nowhere for me to go. Nowhere to hide. Their tall thin form seems to ripple out of the darkness towards me.

"Long time no see, Lil." A low, menacing growl rumbles from the shadows, sending fear straight down my spine. The air grows thicker and heavier with each terrified pant. I fight against my blurring vision as adrenaline takes over.

"Adam."

29

Samael

It's been over twenty-four hours since Lily went missing. Everyone has been working around the clock to find her. Not even Levi was able to come up with any traces of her on surveillance. Manny established new shifts with his employees. Michael's team has come up empty. It amazes me that with the entire strength of the police force out there searching for her, they have found no trace of her whatsoever. Not even a single lead on her whereabouts. What good are they if they can't find her?

At this point, there is only one person left to go to for help. The cold air fills my lungs, calming me as I place my hand on the door handle. This is it. There's no turning back now. The bells hanging from the other side of the door ring out. "Twice in a week. That's new. Have you found something else you would like to get your lady friend?" Endora playfully chuckles while pulling candles out of a box and placing them on the shelf before her.

I rub the back of my neck. "No. Actually. I need your help with another matter." Endora's long black casual dress moves like wind is hitting it. "It's not what you think. Lily is missing. She's been gone for a few days."The dress settles and Endora stands tall. "I've come to make a deal."

Endora's jaw drops. "You want to make a deal with me? What's the catch?" It's understandable that she would be cautious about cutting a deal. The contracts I have written over the span of my existence always come with a price to pay.

"No catch. I need you to do a location spell to find Lily, and in return," I force out, square my shoulders in resolution. "I will owe you a favor." Endora's head raises slightly as she narrows her eyes. I have never owed anyone. I believed that it wouldn't happen. However, this situation is different. I'm different. To care about someone other than myself is new and wild. She is worth more than my pride.

Endora doesn't say a word. She just stands there and stares at me. I can feel her eyes peering into my soul, searching for my intentions. There's no reason to resist. I open myself up to her, allowing Endora to search my energy until she is satisfied. This will fail if she doesn't trust that I am authentic in what I speak. After what feels like an eternity of intense perusal, she finally relaxes and says,"Fine, but I will hold onto your debt until I truly require your assistance." Endora heads to her back room.

I let out a deep sigh and close myself off again. This was easier than I thought it would be. Although, being the only person in history to own a debt on me is a lucrative price. "Are you coming?" A click comes from the front door. Without assistance, the open sign hanging on the door flips over, closing the shop to the public. I guess this requires more privacy than I understood.

Stepping over the barrier between the shop and her sacred

space drains me. I don't think I will ever get used to that feeling. The dimly lit room has the same heavy air of an otherworldly aura. The flickering candles casting shadows across the wet, aged logs covered in moss seem brighter than before. As I step through the threshold, I find an extravagant round table in the center of the room that is covered in various runes and colors. "Do some remodeling?"

Endora lays down a considerably sized map of the area that takes up most of the table. "No. I have this space enchanted so that way if anyone does somehow make it back here, they look past the important things. Since I now have you by the balls, it's not necessary to keep you completely in the dark." Endora grabs four white candles and pillars, placing them at the four corners of the map. Endora then takes a small cauldron full of powder and walks clockwise around us, sprinkling the mixture onto the floor.

As the circle is completed, Endora raises her hands and begins chanting, "I call upon the guardians of the watchtower of the North. We come to you seeking clarity and truth. Hear us. I call to you, the guardians of the watchtower of the East. We come to you to cleanse this space of deception and hate. Hear us. I call to you, the guardians of the watchtower of the South. We come to you for healing and to regenerate our weary souls. Hear us. I call to you the guardians of the watchtower of the West. Purify and transform this space so that we may find the answers we seek. Hear us." The powder circle Endora cast around us begins to glow. Holy shit.

Endora then drops her arms from the heavens and stretches them out to each side.

"Point to where you saw her last," she instructs without looking at me. I hold my breath, captivated by the map before me. The once-static lines begin to writhe and pulse as swirling constellations and ancient symbols appear on the paper. It pulses with an otherworldly energy and brings definition to each symbol with each bound. Colorful mountains grow from the page outlining the valley we live in. Buildings rise up in their muted brick and stone with identical textures. The sound of a car crash comes from the northern edge of the paper.

"Where did you get this?" It's as if the entire city is alive in it. People walking, cars moving up and down streets, even the occasional bird comes into view. The map is just as alive as the real world. No, it is the world.

"Focus. If your head and heart aren't fully in this, it won't work," Endora cautions, her tone bristling with frost before gentling as she continues. "Find where you saw her last and then channel every last ounce of emotion you have for this woman. See her in your mind as clearly as possible." I follow the route from Endora's Occult Shop to my house.

I know a little more about Endora, and now she is going to know where I live. Normally, I would be more cautious, but this is not the time. I have to trust Endora. She is my last hope. I place my finger on my house. "Here." Despite the map looking like a live recording from an aerial view, it still feels like paper. A shimmering X appears on the map under my finger.

When I pull my hand away, I focus every ounce of energy I have available and think of Lily. My heart swells and my chest grows warm with a gentle flutter. Memories of every glance we've exchanged sends a rush of electricity through my veins. I think about her smile. I adore her smile. How her face lights up, and in turn, she lights my world in a passionate blaze that refuses to cease. When she curls her body into mine,

I'm enveloped in a cocoon of pure bliss. Lily's signature floral scent is burnt in my memory so deeply that I swear she is right next to me. Each moment spent in her presence is a gift that I can never repay.

Whenever I'm with her, it's as if the entire world fades away. It's only us. Picturing her touch ignites a fire within me, spreading through my core with untamable devotion. Lily understands me for who I am. It's something else to finally be accepted by the right person. No matter how much she hates it, her laugh is like music to my ears. I read a poem once that said you shouldn't build a house out of people but, with Lily, it's as if I've found my home in her arms.

"Gracious ones more than me, I ask you to show what is unseen. From darkest nights to brightest days, show us where our friend Lily lies. As I say, SO MOTE IT BE." The sound of lightning claps through the room. As if being struck by it, the map ignites before us. Flames spark up across the map, casting away every thread of darkness this room contained.

Power like this only comes once in a century. I've trusted my debt to the right collector. I'm honored to work with the witch Endora. As the flames recede, I cautiously step closer and inspect the map. The X that marks where my house is still there.

"She's right here." Endora points to the map, leading my sight to a charred spot well across town. All of those flames and only this little section is singed. The rest of the map appears untouched.

I go to work, memorizing every turn that separates me from her. "Thank you," I murmur, making an attempt to express my sincere gratitude even while dedicating Lily my attention to discerning Lily's whereabouts. Endora walks around the table to my side. I don't move. I need to make sure I get there. "Wait. I know this. I know exactly where this is."

I swear we had sent someone to that location. It was one of the first places I told Manny to send his men. "Can I make a call in here?" Endora nods. When Manny answers the phone, I don't give him the time to speak. "Did you or did you not send people to check Adam Genesis's house when I told you to?"

He rumbles, "Of course I did." Papers shift over the line.

"I'm going to give you one more chance to figure your story out." I hang up the phone and slip it into my pocket. Endora stands there muttering under her breath. "Open the circle now." Endora's face goes blank. The power she wields pulsing in waves around her. Her eyes fade into dark voids. As she gets close, the sacred circle begins to gleam and black flames flare to life along its edges, trapping us inside.

Endora grabs hold of my face and begins speaking in an ethereal voice. "Samael, Prince of Lies, Father of Sin, Deceiver of Souls, The Most Unclean, I bless you with strength from the unseen. Let it sit inside your chest so you may use it to begin my quest. Godly light simmering true, the nature of battle courses within you. Twist and tie this burning light, given freely for its might. Final step of my seeds sown. Ancient revenge shall unfold." Endora's hand rips open by an invisible force, spilling her blood onto the floor. It comes out like black sludge. "Take my offering, hear my plea, as I say it so mote it be!"

Every muscle in my body gets painfully tight. The blood on the floor begins to bubble. I try to step back but I am frozen in place. Two black snakes crawl out of the puddle and head to my feet. I can't even move my head to watch them. However,

I can feel their weight on my legs as they coil around me in unison. It's both relaxing and unsettling.

As they make their way to my chest, the pressure grows. I can feel them push into my sternum through my skin. If I could scream, I would. The searing pain is almost too much. I can feel them move around inside of me. My chest grows tighter and tighter. They must be wrapping around my heart.

"Good luck." Endora utters sincerely. She puts two fingers out, and the circle opens, allowing me to move.

30

Lily

The pain is nearly unbearable. Every square inch of my body throbs relentlessly. Throughout the night, my body has become a battleground where agony reigns supreme. Between Adam and this fucking psycho woman tossing me down here to begin with, I have endured more pain than I ever imagined my body could withstand. I know what book she wants. They will have to pry its location from my cold, dead lips. I can finally repay Mr. M for everything he has done for me. My life is a price I am willing to pay.

Each movement is a skirmish, every breath a struggle against the weight of exhaustion. It presses down on me like a suffocating blanket. The only thing that is keeping me grounded is the necklace hidden in my bra. I can focus on it and distract myself from this madness. Adam has taken every opportunity to show me how demented he really is.

He's different. His hits are more brutal. He moves faster than before. He hasn't shown a shred of humanity through the night. Adam even comes across as different. In between his banter, I was able to catch some of the differences. Round scars the size of a half dollar sit at the center of each of his hands. At the crown of his head, an irregular zig-zag line of small red dots mar his skin before disappearing behind his hairline.. His eyes are hollow, as if he had witnessed a terror beyond comprehension.

"What happened to you?" I whisper softly, struggling to form words against the battery of pain that seizes my body demanding attention. With all to few breaks in this seemingly endless cycle of torture, a moment of repreive is needed. If I get him talking then not only can I get a moment of rest, but I can learn if he's broken or this is all a game.

My limbs feel heavy, laden with fatigue. It seeps into my bones and settles there like an unwelcome guest. "You would never believe me," he scoffs. The rasp in his voice is new. It isn't just the harshness of his tone that bites me, but the coldness devoid of emotion.

Pushing my body up off the ground is like wading through quicksand. "Try me. It's not like I have anything else to do right now. For old times' sake," I grunt, shuffling my arms closer to me. My arms plea for mercy as they bear my full weight, dragging me deeper and deeper into a quagmire of weariness. I don't know how much more of this I can take.

Adam stands up and walks across the room towards me. Flinching back, a bolt of pain shoots through my body, a fierce reminder of my newfound limitations. "You really want to know?" he questions softly. Through labored breaths, I nod my head. "That night I marked you as mine forever, someone came into the house. I ran and hid in the spare bedroom. I expected them to leave, and I could get back to finish you off, and then I heard him." His gaze drifts off to the distance. An invisible veil of darkness paints his face.

It's obvious that despite being physically here, mentally Adam is entirely somewhere else. "He told me that God had called him to punish me. That what I did was wrong. Smoke started curling in from under the door, and then it got quiet. So…quiet." his voice trails off. There's no mistaking what night he is referring to. A noose of emotion wraps around my neck as the memory creeps in. The last night I was in that house before the fire. The night he raped me.

Just thinking the word twists my stomach. I don't remember any of the story he is telling me, but I will never forget what he did to me. "When I saw him, I couldn't look away. There were flames everywhere. H-he had these giant wings shooting out of his back. There was nothing human about him. He didn't even touch me. I started to float in the air. T-t-then the screaming, so much screaming." A wave of satisfaction moves through me at his fear. Knowing that he didn't leave that night without some sort of retribution is almost just as good as doing it myself.

My passive triumph is quickly replaced with confusion as my mind picks apart his retelling. A prickling sensation crawls across my skin. My dream. That thing was in my dream."It came from everywhere. So m-much pain, and then it all went quiet. My mind became numb to it all." The hallway was consumed by flames. If he had seen that creature from my nightmares, that would mean…it wasn't a nightmare at all. "He turned around and just left. I thought I would just be hanging there mid-air and bleed to death."

I don't even know how I got out of that house. The world tilts on its axis as I put the pieces together. I remember the darkness that came over me. How my suffering became muted as I stared at the ceiling. I was so cold and numb that I felt like

I was dying…I was dying.

"Do you know what it was?" I pry, hoping that maybe he has an answer. I woke up at Sam's house in his bed. There is an entire chunk of my memory gone. I was unconscious for days, maybe even a week.

Amid the darkness of pain and exhaustion, a flicker of defiance refuses to be resolved in Adam's eyes. Memories of Sam flood me. He nursed me back to health, kept his distance, and told me that he knew everything I needed. The mask he chose for himself at the club. He didn't blink when I fucked every living thing there. Asmodeus. They told me they knew more about Sam. "He said he was the Devil."

The sound of my heart beating deafens me as the realization hits. It's as if reality itself has materialized into a forceful hand, smacking me across the face and leaving the lingering imprint of shock and disbelief. There's an instant where time seems to freeze, suspended in the air as I grapple with the impact of the fact that I know who did this to Adam. The sting of truth resonates through me, sending my stomach to weigh heavily.

I know this creature biblically. There is no denying it. Samael. My sweet, charming, pain in the ass Sam is actually the ultimate bad guy. The singular person you're told to stay away from. The single individual the entire universe blames for every bad thing that ever happens. My Sam. It all makes sense. He wasn't lying to me. I thought it was a joke when he said it. That psycho woman even said that I took from the Devil. For fucks sakes he's a lawyer! It wasn't just a figure of speech. This is how he knew about me. This is the reason he has so much power and so much control.

Satan himself was cast out of heaven, and I landed straight into his bed. A moment of dizziness washes over me. The metallic tang of blood takes over my senses. Though, through this wave of agony a single thought replays in my mind: If Sam is truly the Devil, then he's coming for me.

The pendant pulses against my skin, as hope grows within me. A surge of heat from the pendant clashes with my chilled body. It wasn't keeping me warm, it's a reminder of the strength I have inside of me. With a ragged breath, I cling to the pendant with every last fucking ounce of strength I can muster.

Each hour I survive this hell is a testament to my own resilience. Every breath is a silent vow to these fuckers that I will continue to endure. Even amid all this pain and exhaustion, I find a truth I can cling to. I've consumed Sam's lust, I hold his heart, and I am the only person who has the power to do those things. The strength I need to keep going isn't through other people. It's right here…within me.

"I think it's about time to finish what we started, Lil. Now that my mistress has saved me, no one can stop me." Adam proclaims, breaking my stream of thought.

A torrent of impacts from Adam comes at uncanny speed, overwhelming my senses with a relentless onslaught of batters and blows. My thoughts swirl in a dizzying whirlpool, each one more disjointed and irrational than the last. Deranged laughter fills the room. My laughter. Reality blurs at the edges, twisting and distorting this nightmare.

Steely resolve takes over what little uncertainty was left. A current of uncontrollable, manic laughter claws out of my throat. Adam stands there, just watching me, his lips twitching with rage. "Fuck you and your stupid bitch. You have no idea who the hell you're messing with!" I threaten through my twisted cackle. Adam sends a heavy kick to my gut that pushes the air from my chest, silencing me for only a second.

The room fills with the demonic melody of my own making. A primal urge takes hold of what's left of my shattered consciousness. Driving me towards complete insanity. "I will not be your plaything anymore, Adam!" The frenzy of emotions I've kept bottled up inside expands. The fear, anger, despair, and hopelessness all blend in a baneful elixir that fuels my madness.

Adam picks me up off the ground and throws me across the room. The air is forced out of me again as I abruptly meet the wall. There's no escape. There is no serenity. I scream. The guttural cry of anguish and frustration echoes in the empty recesses of my fractured psyche and out of me.

The taste of iron pools in my mouth. Pulling my legs under me, I resist the temptation to succumb to my agony as I stand. There's no going back. I let my mind fall entirely into the void of insanity. Surrendering to its hypnotic embrace. Bathing in this sea of chaos that was made for me. I spit the blood out onto the unforgiving floor. My muscles cry out while squaring my shoulders. The pendant pulses against my chest, more energetic than before. "Is that the best you got?"

31

Samael

I burst through the charred doorway of Lily's old house. The smell of rot that fills the air chokes me. The remnants of this house that has caused so much torment to my beloved Goddess lie in ruins around me. Here it lies, a decrepit wasteland consumed by the flames of my own creation. My heart races as I navigate through the debris.

A swarm of flies assaults me as I make my way into the old living room. A man's body lays across the floor, surrounded by a puddle of dried blood. His black uniform is proof enough that Manny did send someone here. No wonder I wasn't informed where she was sooner. The poor bastard died.

I catch a glimpse of movement in the corner of my eye. I chase it through the ruins. My footsteps echoing off the crumbling walls and scattered wood. The air is so thick with dust that it swirls around my vision. "Get over here, you fucking coward, and face me like a man!" The shadows flit around the corner. I dart through obstacles of fallen beams and debris, chasing them.

My heart lurches as the floor gives way beneath me. The

disorienting sensation of falling churns my stomach, nauseating me. I reach out, attempting to grab ahold of anything to prevent me from going any further. Air rushes past me, whipping my hair and clothes around.

With a sudden, unyielding impact, I hit the floor. My breath is knocked out of me, and agonizing pain explodes through my body. I have no choice but to lay there for a moment, dazed and confused. The world around me spins in a dizzying blur.

Slowly, I push myself off the floor. My legs tremble at the effort. With a shaky breath, I stand up straight. As the dust settles, I start to make out my surroundings. Scattered rocks and charred pieces of wood litter the dirt ground. Light filters in from the hole above me and a small window on the side. It's evident that either this is new, or it is a service cellar that is not intended to be easily accessible.

Other than this gaping hole, there doesn't seem to be another way out. There isn't much down here either. As I make my way to the back of the room, the glint of metal catches my eye. The ground crunching under my shoes as I go towards it. An unsettling feeling washes over me with the realization that there is a broken chain lying on the ground. The tattered scrap of rubber coating, coated with dust and muck, lays limply on the ground. A solitary chain link, twisted and jagged, hangs off a shredded strip of dark leather. "No," my voice quivers in disbelief.

I notice a warped buckle laying in the dirt beside it and my heart pauses for a single beat. For once, I pray that my imagination is getting the better of me. I follow the chain back to its end, which connects to a blood-stained wall. Bile creeps up my throat. She was here. This must be hers. The more I frantically search, the more blood I find covering the floor and sprayed across the walls and ceiling.

"Like what I did to the place?" a deep, raspy voice says from behind me. A thin tawny man smiles at me, his jade green eyes sparkling with malicious glee beneath his wavy brown hair. Adam. How is this motherfucker still alive? "Taking Lily was just the bait I needed to get you alone. I can't take all the credit. My mistress came up with the plan. She's been watching you two closely," he says nonchalantly. I can hear my teeth click as I grind them against each other.

"Well, that explains how you survived. If I recall correctly, I had left you to die here," I jeer motioning to our surroundings. "Now, I get to kill you a second time." My knuckles burn from clenching my fists so tight. I want to feel his life leave his body with my bare hands. No powers, no magic, just a bare knuckle brawl.

"My mistress had other plans for me. You see, it turns out that this little arrangement my mistress and I have works out in both our favor. She gets Lily." In an instant, Adam and I are nose to nose. "And I get you." his voice low and gravely.

Adam suddenly delivers a flurry of blows to my abdomen and chest. His unnatural speed and sheer strength take me by surprise. He was not like this the last time we met. He was a weak, cowardly human. I leap back, Adam meeting my pace. It takes most of my concentration to dodge his punches. He's methodical and chaotic all at the same time.

I laugh in his face. "You give every impression that your mistress made a poor choice when choosing you." I was right to assume I wouldn't be making it out of here alive. "Tell me. How is Ali doing these days?" I ask steadily while dodging another fist heading for my cheek. Adam smiles, sharp canines peeking out from behind his lips.

I take the opportunity to deliver a sharp jab to his ribs. It lands with a satisfying thud but Adam barely flinches. He retaliates with an uppercut that grazes my jaw. As I stumble back, I call out to my shadows, commanding them to rip every sin from Adam and deliver them to me.

"She's well." he replies, the calmness of his voice at odds with the struggle unfolding between us. His words become more taunting as he continues, "She said you were a waste of her time, and I can have you all to myself. Though she was kind and let me finish what you interrupted." A single bead of sweat falls down Adams face as he steps back a pace, his eyes looking around towards my shadows.

A furious scream escapes me. "I'm going to kill you, and this time there is no coming back!" Flames erupt from the ground once more, illuminating the entirety of the space. The skin on my back rips open, allowing my wings full length to show themselves. My shadows whip around at chaotic speed.

A surge of power courses through me as I unfurl my wings. With a deafening whoosh, they slice through the air, propelling me forward with the force of a catapult. Like a feathered arrow, I shoot towards Adam, my form a blur of speed and determination.

With a primal roar, I snatch him in my grip and haul him towards the ceiling. The air ripping past my ears as I drag him through the open space of the basement, his body becomes a ragdoll in my grasp. With a sickening thud, I throw him into the unforgiving wall. The concrete behind him explodes in a shower of dust and debris, leaving an Adam sized crater where his back makes contact.

"We are more alike than you think, Satan." A ragged cough rips through Adam, punctuated by a metallic tag as he wipes a crimson line from his cracked lip. Despite being blood stained, defiance glistens in his eyes. I descend from the air, each beat of my wings stirring dust around my feet. My steps, like a predator closing in on its wounded prey. The space between us crackles with a tension so thick I can taste it.

"We are nothing alike," I snarl, a thrill of victory searing through me as I spot a weakness in his defense. We trade blows, grappling, and wrestling within the confined space. The air is thick with the sounds of our labored breathing, the raging flames surrounding us, and the thuds of each of our exchanged blows. I take the opening and pound my fist into Adam's chest.

For a moment, Adam goes limp in my hands. My shadows rip through him one by one, delivering me splinters of his soul. His skin pales as blood spills from his mouth. "I'm much worse." Without a sound I wrestle him to his feet. His body, a dead weight a moment ago, twitches with a final spark of defiance. But defiance won't save him from my wrath. Gripping his arm like a vice, I hurl him with a sickening heave. Adam screams a brief desperate cry. He arches through the air, landing within the inferno and remains motionless as the hellfire surrounding us begins to consume his flesh.

I call back my shadows and like tendrils they slither across the floor, vanishing beneath my feet. My silhouette, stark and menacing against the illuminated ground, sways with the flames dancing. Lily. I won't leave this forsaken place without her. The very air thickens with my determination and my silent vow echoing in the emptiness.

The inferno raging around me casts an eerie, flickering glow as it climbs up to the collapsing basement ceiling. The flames reveal more of the space than before, casting long, distorted shadows around the room. I inch closer, tracing the chain link by link back towards the source, my senses on high alert. Suddenly a glint- a detail I'd missed before- snags my eye, freezing me in place. An oblong mound of soil is heaped in the corner of the room. My mouth runs dry. No.

I rush over to it, dropping to my knees, and dig. Pushing pile after pile of soil, my heart races with anticipation, mingling with this sense of dread that gnaws at my insides. "Please be alive. Please be alive." With another swipe, a sliver of grayed skin peeks out. No.

A breath catches in my throat as I carefully move the soil away, revealing a nose. As more of the face is revealed, a strangled gasp escapes my lips, taking in the sight before me. "Goddess." Time stands still as I dig her out, every handful of soil heavy with disbelief. I refuse to accept what I am seeing. "I got you, Goddess. Give me a few more seconds. I'll get you out of this."

It's just a cruel trick that Adam is playing on me. She is not gone. She isn't. Frantically, I dig her out entirely and drag Lily's heavy, motionless corpse onto my lap. My hands tremble as I swipe away remnants of the dirt from her face. "Come on, Lily. Wake up." I pinch her nose and swipe down to clear the compacted soil within her nostrils.

Tears stream down my face. My voice cracks. "Wake up, Goddess. Wake up." I place my first two fingers on her neck, searching for a pulse. When I can't find it, I pull her closer to me and listen to her chest. Nothing. I hear nothing. The reality of the situation washes over me like a tidal wave of grief and disbelief. She's gone. I was too late.

I pull her body closer to me and hold her tightly, rocking back and forth, "I'm sorry, I'm so sorry. I failed you. Lily."

There is no holding it back. Memories of us flood my mind. She can't be gone. I gaze up to the heavens. "Please. I'll do anything. Don't do this to me. Don't take her. Take me! Take me instead!"

I hold onto her tighter, laying my head on top of hers as I stroke her hair. A river of tears continues to flow. I don't know how long I sit there with her in my arms, before I notice a small section of Lily's chest has grown warm. I lean Lily's body back and find a golden shimmer emanating from the inside of her shirt.

I reach into her shirt and pull out a glowing pendant. I inspect it carefully, brushing my fingers across the smooth metallic surface. "How did you get this?" I realize it's the pendant I had Endora search for sitting in my hand. Hope swells within me. "Forgive me, Goddess." I place the pendant onto the center of Lily's chest and kiss her on the forehead. "I would ask for permission, but you need to eat, and I will not take no for an answer. Take it. Take it all from me. Every last drop."

With full force, I kiss her cold, soil-covered lips. The earthy taste of dirt fills my mouth as I sweep my tongue in her mouth. Tears continue to stream down my face. Take it, Lily. Wake up and take it from me. This will work. I know it will work. The pendant burns under my hand as I hold it to her chest.

Lily's eyes shoot open as she grabs me by the throat. I won't stop. I refuse to stop. Take it all from me. The whites of her eyes gradually fade into an endless black void. From the roots, inky streaks spread through her bright chestnut hair, gradually transforming it to match her eyes. Lily's beautiful chestnut hair transforms into a shimmering onyx. She starts to kiss me back in a feral way that she has never done before.

"Consume me whole. I give up all of myself for you to live," I pledge earnestly. Suddenly, my throat constricts. A startling, unexplainable sensation stirs deep within my core, pulling my focus from Lily. Panic grows as I gag at the bile brushing across my tongue.

Lily pushes me slowly away from her. I continue to gag at the feeling of something slowly being pulled out of my throat. When I am an arm's length away from her, I witness the snakes that Endora had forced within me curling out of my mouth and into hers.

Lily stands up and leers down at me with untamed hunger. I remain on my knees, throwing my arms open, fully offering myself to my Goddess. As she takes in the last of the snakes, my hellfire changes to black flames. My own shadows abandon me and shroud her in their ethereal bodies. My Dark Goddess. My vision quickly tunnels, restricting my sight to only her. You're so beaut-

32

Lilith

Sam falls to the ground motionless with a loud thud.

"Well, don't you look precious. I gotta give it to ya, Lil. I thought once I drained you of every last drop, there would be no coming back from that. I guess we get to have a little more fun after all. Speaking of fun, did you like how I buried you? That was Mistress' idea. She really wanted to fuck with this guy's head. Something about making him feel the loss that she felt." A fire burns deep in my belly just listening to Adam's taunting voice.

I retrieve my pendant from where it has fallen to the ground and tie it around my neck. Its metal is heavy and cold on my skin. I know I should feel something as I stare at Sam's lifeless corpse lying on the ground. There is nothing left in him. Just a useless meat suit. "Honestly, babe, what did you see in that guy? It was his money, wasn't it? I mean the actual devil. Can you get any lower?" Adam groans.

I watch as Adam saunters closer. His desire and lust radiate around his charred body. He cocks his head and kicks at Sam's lifeless body. "What a worthless piece of shit. Couldn't even handle kissing you. You just have a way of killing everyone in your life, don't you? Your mom, your aunt, your sister, me, and now this fucker." Adam picks up a beam of wood from the ground as he jests. My knuckles ache.

Every joint in my body cracks as I stand more erect. My skin doesn't feel the same on my body. Once I'm at full height, I settle into myself. I don't just feel different. I feel lethal. "What, no reply? Not a single rebuttal? Stupid fucking cunt. Cat got your tongue again? I can fix that just like I did last time." Adam draws back the two-by-four he holds and swings it toward my side. The wood splinters across my hand as I go to push it away.

Adam's brows go taut as his head darts back and forth between the broken wood in his hand and me. Wind begins to stir from the ground up. It starts as a gentle whisper brushing against my skin. Its subtle caress is barely noticeable at first, but as it builds, the wind tightens around me. Adam's hair and singed clothes move around him, warning him of the tempest to come.

A somber rumble vibrates through the air from behind me. "For the crimes that you have committed against the women who came before me," my voice booms. I reach my hands down, and short coarse fur passes under them. Two tan lionesses walk around me. One clockwise, the other counterclockwise, rubbing their massive bodies against my skin. There is no fear with them. I bend down and scratch the one to my right.

A strong feminine voice echoes in my mind. "I am Ultio. I seek your revenge, Mother." It sits down, staring at Adam. The lioness to my left takes her place on the opposite side of me. "I am Iustitia. Let me be your justice, Mother." In unison, the lionesses thunderously roar. I sense their strength and ferocity.

My spine tingles at their proclamation. The wind picks up, and dirt pulls up from the ground, creating a fantastical whirlwind about the room. The fires around us grow. A weighted sensation threatens to pull me back. I am not weak. I will not falter. "For the crimes you have committed against the women who came after me."

It's as if I have another set of arms. I stretch them out, discovering large black wings. The feathers are massive, angled at sharp points. They are beautiful. The wind howls and whistles, and the black flames around us thwap along with it, creating a symphony of indignation.

Adam fumbles back slightly, fighting to get closer to me. "The whore gets the devil's dick wet and thinks she is invincible. I've marked you as mine! There is no coming back from this! You will always remember what it feels like to have my hands on your skin! You will never forget what it feels like to have me inside of you! I. *Own.* You."

Two long black snakes push out of my belly, curling up and around my body. As they make their way to my head, I feel my hair being pulled up. The dark serpents settle at my crown with gentle pressure. "For the crimes you have committed against me." The lionesses roar once again. They stand up and lean down, preparing to pounce.

Adam steps into the eye of my storm. A smug grin grows across his face. I lean down and get close to his ear. I whisper, "I commend your soul to the darkest corner of my kingdom." The smell of fear and adrenaline permeates from him. With a primal roar, Ultio and Iustitia launch themselves forward. Adam is thrown to the ground in a blur of fur and sinew.

Their attack is breathtaking. Each one of them clawing and biting at Adam's flailing body with lethal grace. A mist of warm liquid hits my face, as he is ripped limb from limb. His blood spatters around the space, staining the lioness's fur crimson. Commanding the shadows that shroud me, they move, gathering Adam's sins as Ultio and Iustitia finish him off. His agony is music to my ears.

A translucent apparition of Adam stands above his body. He looks down at himself, and his mouth opens as though he is screaming, yet nothing is heard. The winds pick up at breathtaking speed, forming a cyclone around us. "Goodbye, Adam."

Adam's apparition is picked up in the wind, spinning around the room. A deafening sound of buzzing replaces the noise of the wind. The cyclone tightens, receding into the ground. Adam is pulled with it. The lionesses bite into his corpse, making a deep, crunching sound as his skull is shattered underneath their strong jaws. The apparition of Adam tries to grab onto everything, his arms passing through the solid surfaces.

With the final wisp of him disappearing into the earth, the fires and winds recede. Ultio and Iustitia purr while they consume the remainder of his body. I stroke their fur gently. "Thank you for your assistance." Iustitia picks her head up, licking the blood from her muzzle.

Iustiria's voice is solid and steady in my mind. "It is our pleasure to serve you, Mother." I grab both sides of her massive head and press my forehead to hers. Iustiria's purr deepens, reverberating through my body. As I let go, she passes her sharp, sandpaper-like tongue across my face.

The shadows flit to Sam's motionless body lying on the floor in a way that I can only interpret as panic. To settle them, I walk over and watch as they move around him. Sam's massive wingspan takes up much of this corner of the room. His beauty is almost painful. It's only now that I can see him for who he truly is. Sam was never human. He cloaked himself so well that missing the apparent sharp angles of his jaw and heavenly-crafted perfection was easy through mortal eyes.

The dirt digs into my knees as I kneel next to him. "Live." The shadows come together and funnel into his mouth in a thin stream of darkness. Sam's chest rises slowly. Reaching out, I pluck a shadow from the stream and consume it. I let it sit inside me momentarily as it gathers my own sin and the remaining pieces of Sam that brought me back.

When the last of the funnel enters him, I lean down and gingerly press my lips to his. Forcing the consumed shadow out of me and feeding Sam. His piercing blue eyes flutter open. "Good morning, sleepy head." I coo lovingly while giving him a moment to wake up.

Sam grabs me by the back of the neck and pulls me in. Our lips meet in a feverish embrace, igniting a blaze of passion that consumes us both. There's a desperate urgency in the way our bodies press together.

After a moment of losing ourselves in one another, Sam pulls away, his breath ragged and his expression pained. "I thought I lost you." Tears stream down Sam's face. Every touch sends shivers down my spine, and my wings settle close against me until they disappear out of my vision.

Sam searches my face as if trying to convince himself this isn't a dream. "I'm sorry I lied to you. I'm sorry I didn't get here faster." Sam places a quick kiss on my face with each apology. The weight of longing lifts off my shoulders as I remember what I felt for this man.

With each fervent kiss, I sense my form becoming smaller. The wings recede back within my flesh. The serpents climb down from my crown, wrapping themselves around my neck, adding to the leather cord. At this moment, nothing else matters but the fiery connection between us. This sweet relief from the chaos of the world around us. "All is forgiven. I know now why life had to happen this way."

The lionesses rumble from behind Sam. He sits up quickly and moves his body in a way that shields me from them. My heart swells and I giggle at the sight. Pushing his arm away, I walk around him to Ultio and Iustitia, this time holding onto Ultio and pressing my head onto hers. The lioness settles into a purr. "Lily. How? What?"

I kiss Ultio's nose and laugh at Sam's dropped jaw. I slowly close his mouth and wipe off the blood from the corner of his lips. "Turns out there's a new badass in town. Now, take me home, ya little Devil. Your Goddess requires your service." Sam stands from the ground, brushing off some of the dirt that coats his pants.

He lowers his head and bows down. "As you wish." When he lifts his head, that mischievous grin is painted on his face. This is going to be fun. He rushes closer to me, sweeping me up in his arms. With each beat, his wings make a loud thwump, lifting us from the ground and out of this God-forsaken place.

A single tear escapes me as I watch as Ultio and Iustitia vanish into the shadows. "By the way." I smack Sam on the shoulder. "That's for dying on me, asshole."

Once we are out of the basement, Sam puts me on the ground and grabs my hand leading me to the door. "Well then, since we both died and came back to life, allow me to properly introduce myself. I am Samael, Prince of Lies, Father of Sin, Deceiver of Souls, The Most Unclean, Lucifer of the Morningstar, and I am wildly in love with you, Lily." Sam kisses the back of my hand.

As I open the front door , Sam and I walk through the threshold. The deathly scent of fall in full bloom, reminds me that I am no longer feeble and weak. This is just the beginning. A faint melodic whisper catches my ear as we walk to the car. While no words can be made out, I understand it completely. "No, Lily is dead," I say in a low voice. Sam gives me a side-glance, his eyebrows scrunching together.

"Well then, what shall I call my Goddess?" One of Sam's eyebrows raises and a cockeyed smile sits on his face.

The whisper comes again, filling me with a sense of purpose. "Lilith," I introduce myself proudly and in that moment, I know exactly what I'm meant to do.

As long as I am alive.

As long as I roam the earth.

I will seek revenge and justice for people who have suffered like I had.

I will answer their silent prayers that have gone unheard.

Through me, they will be able to stand in their truth, embrace their darkness, and leave fear behind so that passion may grow.

For the flames of chaos are within us all.

33

Lilith

inter.

"Hot. Hot. Hot." Sam laughs at me as I put my London Fog back onto the table. I'm so thankful everything has gone right back to normal. Saint Drogo Roasters is still and will always be, by far, my favorite place to get a cup of tea in town... other than Mr. M's, of course.

I do not know what that man does differently than everyone else in the universe to make such a damn good cup. Sam, however, still needs to work on his brewing abilities. He recently picked up this cute little frother and has been attempting to make fancy tea art.

"Hey. Be careful, it's hot." Sam deadpans, taking a sip of his coffee. I think if I roll my eyes one more time today, I'm going to strain them.

"No shit, Sherlock. Tell me something I don't already know." I groan, grabbing a napkin off the table to clean up the bit of tea that spilled on the table. Moving in with Sam permanently is the best idea I have had in a long time. With Sam's help, I was able to get a job at the local women's shelter. Sam has been talking about volunteering his time to take on some of the cases. His efforts are going towards his pro-bono hours.

There, I can make real change. Show the women that they can be safe and someone out there does care, and if it so happens, their abusers get out of hand, well, they have another thing coming. I won't let these people suffer alone. I know what that feels like. Besides, I'm sure Ultio and Iustitia would be happy to go out on their own and hunt.

"Are you stopping by Mr. M's today?" Sam asks suddenly, prompting me to pull out my phone to check the time. I pull out my phone to check the time. Shit, I got to go. I was supposed to be there an hour ago. I toss my things into my purse. Sam grabs my tea, pouring it into a to-go cup. "Hal and I will be by later tonight to pick you up. Don't forget that we are going to be seeing Asmodeus tonight."

Grabbing my cup from his hand, I give Sam a quick peck, and dash towards the door. "What the fuck was that woman?" he demands from behind me, sounding simultaneously amused and stern. "Come over here and give me a real kiss." Yup, my eyes are definitely going to get stuck this way.

I flip around and painfully smoosh our lips together haphazardly. "You're lucky I love you." I beam. Sam licks the side of my face, leaving a trail of spit behind. Disgusted, I wipe it off. "There is something seriously wrong with you."

"Nope. If I lick it, then it's mine. I licked you. You're now mine," he declares smugly, his entire demeanor radiating satisfaction. I will never understand this man.

"Well, then, you better get to licking something else later tonight before I let someone else get the first taste." Sam lets out a husky growl that makes me want to clench my thighs together. Before he convinces me to change my mind with that devilish glare of his, I run out of the shop and make my way to the best-adopted dad ever.

This life isn't so bad. I mean, what more can a girl ask for? I got the guy of my dreams. I have friends who care about me. It's the perfect little family made up of complete strangers. I guess that's what that saying really means. The blood of the covenant is truly thicker than the waters of the womb.

The town is busy with Christmas around the corner. Decorative lights and snowmen cover porch stoops as inflatable reindeer blow-ups stand proud. A subtle chill moves through the air, stealing away what little warmth is left from autumn. A newfound emptiness replaces the beautiful mosaic of the surrounding foliage, reminding me that like the earth, we each have our season. Yet, somehow the ivy creeping up Mr. M's bookshop resists against change, remaining evergreen.

Bells chime overhead as I step into Mr. M's, bringing joy and wonder to my soul. The possibility of the day grows with the cracking of firewood and the smell of aged vanilla. As usual, Mr. M sits in his reading chair among his life's passions, sipping tea and reading yet another aged text.

His eyes twinkle in the light as he peers up from his book, resembling that of a thin Santa Claus. His tiny bifocals rest near the tip of his nose and a loving smile grows on his face. "Lily, my dear, I was wondering when you would come. I thought you were supposed to be here earlier." The melodious sound of his voice feels so gentle in my ears. I take my jacket and hat off, carefully placing it on the coat rack, which is probably as old as the building.

"Sorry, I'm late. Sam and I went for some tea, and I completely lost track of time." The old floorboards creak from the weight of my step. Mr. M puts the book on the table, stands, and wraps me in his arms.

Mr. M pauses, his brows furrowing in confusion. "I thought you were going to change your hair again." Mr. M speculates, scratching the back of his head. "Eh. I like it this way. It fits you quite nicely." He compliments me with a smile. I brush my onyx hair back behind my ear, his compliment warming me enough to blush.

"Thanks. I like it too. I think I'm going to keep it." There is no way in hell I will ever tell him that it is permanently black now or how I got it. I have to say I actually love it. All the fun of getting a new hair color without the hair dye. Talk about saving time and money!

Spending the day lost in the aisles, helping customers discover new books, or revisiting old favorites is exactly what the doctor ordered. Mr. M shares his passion for literature with everyone. He points out hidden gems and swaps stories of his reading adventure with anyone who asks. With every customer, our bond grows stronger.

In the quiet moments between discussions, I catch glimpses of his well-earned wisdom and kindness that are so obviously shaped by a lifetime of experiences. His laughter fills the air as we share anecdotes and inside jokes, creating memories that will last forever.

The day passes faster than I would like. The only indication I have of it being the end of the day is when Sam and Hal walk into the shop. In between conversations, Sam steals wide-eyed glances at me begging for salvation. Revenge is sweet. You lick my face, and I refuse to free you from the long-winded persiflage of Mr. M. Besides, watching them banter back and forth warms my heart. It's nice to know that they have grown this close.

"Well, since you're not busy, how about I give you this, and then I can get you both out of here," Sam proposes teasingly, interrupting Mr. M mid-quip. Hal takes Sam's place, joining Mr. M in his loving pursuit of mockery and tomfoolery, becoming more relaxed with each successful blow towards Sam's impromptu departure from conversation, letting his unique accent grow more apparent with every verbal riposte. I can only imagine what Sam bought me this time. I take the bag from Sam and head to the back to change.

When I open the paper bag, I find a sleeveless black dress that shines in the light. Its satin fabric feels almost like nothing in my hands. When I slip it on, the dress falls to the floor and practically molds to my hourglass figure. Its V-neckline plummets straight down, ending just below my breasts. The edges of the neckline are covered with black floral adornments that twine together at the vertex of the neckline before trailing down to meet the slit that begins at the top of my hip.

After zipping it up, I put on the tall heels that came with it. With one final check, I make sure my pendant sits precisely on my chest and walk out to meet them. As I enter the room, the soft mumbles of their conversation come to a halt. "Alright, I'm ready to go," I announce enthusiastically.

"Oh, I am definitely making sure I come to the club tonight," Hal declares. Sam slaps Hal in the chest and gives him a stern look. I might be able to eat when I please, but there are some boundaries that shouldn't be crossed. Besides, eating from Hal would just be weird. Hal fixes his golf cap on his head, shrugging his shoulders. "What? Are you blind? She's drop-dead gorgeous!"

My cheeks burn. I know I'm blushing. Sam wraps his arm

around mine. "I'm sorry, sir, but I'm going to have to steal her away. I'll make sure she remembers to stop by on Monday," he promises Mr. M, stoically ignoring Hal's jibes. Sam reaches his hand out and is met by Mr. M. Without final goodbyes, we head to the car.

I pause just outside of the door, taking a moment to appreciate this place and everything it has done for me. Memories of how I had first come here, broken and lonely, flow through me, cementing my feeling that this magical place is a true sanctuary for me.

I guess that part is true, too. Magic can always be found in a bookshop and thisis truly a magical place for me. Who knows what would have happened if I had never stepped foot in here? Mr. M. and his shop gave me respite in a time of chaos. I know now that you can always find hope in the most unexpected places.

34

Cain

The full moon hangs low, casting an eerie glow on the street, once full of life, now deserted. As I walk down the barren street, a cool breeze finds its way through my long trench coat. The hushed world allows for the rhythm of my footsteps to break the silence. I didn't understand why my Mistress wanted me to come to this God-forsaken town, but now that her plan is coming together, I can see it.

Every flicker of movement catches my attention as my heightened senses take me to the final resting place of Mistress Ali's next victim. The distant hum of a lone car pierces the silence of the night, caring little about anyone or anything around it. As I gracefully hunt, searching for the miscreant who stole her grimoire, the street lamps cast long shadows across the pavement. Embracing the solitude of the hour, I wonder, reveling that I, too, am one of the many secrets hidden beneath this moonlit veil.

A wooden sign hangs above an ivy-covered building. The slight gusts of wind coax the wooden sign hanging above to swing, whimpering a high-pitched groan. *Mr. M's Bookshop*

Vintage Volumes and Antiques. Found you. Painted gold lettering on the glass window shines lazily as the fireplace illuminates within. The dancing flames reflecting off the glass emulate the foreboding destruction I will bestow upon it. How fitting.

The door of the bookshop creaks softly as I ease it shut behind me. Not even the bells hanging above me make my presence known. The only sounds are those of the crackling wood at the back of the shop and the occasional turning of pages from the old man sitting before it.

I stop the gently swinging closed sign to conceal my entrance further. Moving like a phantom, my steps barely audible to human ears as I slink my way into the rows of shelves, shrouded in an elegant blanket fit for a predator such as myself. The shelves cast elongated shadows as I blend with the ambiguity of this massive collection.

Flitting from book to book, searching for the title that my Mistress desires. Her words echo in my head.

He stole it from me, and I want it back. You have to get it for me, Love. You want to make your Mistress happy, right? You said you would do anything for me. Without it, I can't see my oath fulfilled. Do this for me, and I will make your wildest dreams come true.

After I get what my Mistress needs, I'll end him. For her. Anything for her.

Sneaking around him within the twilight of the dimly lit space is almost too easy. The air nearly choking me with its musty scent of decaying paper. The rickety shelves are easy enough to move around. The floor stays silent with each step despite being burdened with the weight of forgotten stories.

No one cares about ancient parables or novellas anymore. The passion for wading through anthologies has come to extinction with this new era. So many of the shelves sag with neglect. I'm astonished they haven't collapsed already from the weight. Each book seems to hold its breath as I make my way through each narrow aisle.

Mistress said she needs the grimoire this old man stole from her many years ago. Whatever the Mistress wants, she gets. I'll do anything for her. Without her, I would be nothing or dead like Abel. He didn't have what it takes. He never had what it takes to do the hard thing. Always me. The forgotten child, but not with her. Her favorite. Her chosen.

The wooden floorboards threaten to speak under my misplaced step, begging to protest my intrusion. With the watery glimmer of the fireplace, long shadows dance across the dusty books the closer I get, concealing me better than I could have hoped. Peaking through the shelves, the old man sits reading, utterly oblivious to my presence. His glasses sit at the brim of his nose. *Ba-boom ba-boom ba-boom.* His heart sounds strong enough, but is his mind prepared to witness my Mistress's blessing?

I doubt he would struggle much. His frail body is seemingly ready to give out at any time. Although, I like it when they struggle. Adrenaline makes the blood so much sweeter. The pleasure that comes over me when their crimson blood washes over my tongue. My mouth salivates at the thought. I want more. I need to taste his aged blood. I watch as he gets up from his seat and moves to the shelf I'm behind.

The air around me is still, disturbed only by his presence and the sigh of the leather binding he pulls from the shelf. The brittle yellow pages tucked within crinkle at his touch, as if resenting any attempt at disturbing their eternal slumber. With each turning page, dust drifts lazily in the wan of the firelight, creating a gloomy spectral ballet that goes unnoticed. I doubt his vision is clear enough to see it.

When I'm finished with him, this place will become nothing but a forlorn sanctuary of forgotten knowledge. The books will stand silent and witness my power. With the passage of time, they will be able to wearily decay as their once vibrant tales will be reduced to echoes. Like him, this shop will be a relic of a bygone era, a testament to my cruel indifference to both.

As my eyes lock on to the nape of his neck, the bounding of his veins follows the beating of his heart. My mouth waters even more with anticipation. Running my tongue across my teeth, I'm grounded with the slightest burn of pain as it is sliced. An old grandfather clock rings out the hour.

Ding Ding Ding

As the witching hour is upon us, the old man checks the clock. The beating of his heart speeds up. I will not fail her. I know he can sense me. His innate instincts are surely kicking in. I watch closely while he locks the door. Perfect. No escape. You will give me what she wants.

He walks around the shelves looking. Searching for an answer. Silly old man. You have no idea what is waiting for you. Playing with you is half the fun. I move closer to him, stalking toward my next meal. He whips his head around as if he can feel me getting near.

Ba-boom ba-boom

Ba-boom ba-boom

Ba-boom ba-boom

"Who's there?" He fidgets as his eyes dart around, searching for the unseen danger. Searching for this invisible threat. "I-I have a weapon! Show yourself!" I saunter into the light, revealing myself, laughing.

"We both know that's not true, old man." I smile, showing off my teeth. With a gasp, he stumbles back, falling to the floor. "You have something my Mistress wants, and I intend to leave here with it." He shuffles back, using his hands and heels in an attempt to flee.

"Take it. Anything. Whatever she wants, you can have it. Just don't hurt me,"he pleads, his feeble voice strident with panic. Watching his squirming would be much more entertaining if he could move faster. However, the way he guards himself by hanging his arm over his body is most entertaining. I almost want to pity him for how helpless he is against me. I allow the floor to release its long-awaited groans under my feet, gracefully moving closer.

Ba-boom ba-boom Ba-boom ba-boom
Ba-boom ba-boom Ba-boom ba-boom
Ba-boom ba-boom Ba-boom ba-boom

"I intend to, but I make no promise to leave here without tasting your history first."

Author's Note

clears throat
LOOK MOM!!! I DID IT!!!

Now, with that out of the way, let's actually get this note going.

Dear Reader,

I hope that you have enjoyed my story. If I can say one thing about taking the steps to becoming an author, I would tell you all that it is a learning curve and that curve resembles a circle. There hasn't been a moment during this process that I haven't learned something new.

As many of you may know, there is an entire team that goes behind crafting every story beyond the author. I feel honored to have that team of people and would like to take this time to shout their praise from this proverbial rooftop.

To my Beta and sensitivity readers, thank you for everything you have done to make this book a possibility. Your insight has been a valuable part of this process. I couldn't have asked for a better group of people to be the first to read my story.

To my editor, meeting you must have been divine intervention. Going to the parking lot early to wait for a midnight book release was one of the best decisions I could have made. You have taken the time to teach me new things, accept me for who I am, and, most importantly, be an amazing friend. I need you to take this moment and give yourself a giant pat on the back. Also, from here on out I grant you a never ending supply of Bardic Inspiration. If your DM has a problem with it send him my way!

To my little sister, you have been a light in this never ending tunnel of dreams. Words can not express how important our daily phone calls have been. You have been with me through every step of this process. Thank you for reminding me that I have always been a writer, and that it's time that I start to share my stories with the world. No matter where I am in the world, I can always count on waking up and having a morning chit chat with you.

To my husband, you are the mac to my cheese, the calm in my storm, and the muse that sets my soul free. I can't imagine what my life would look like without you. I said it before and I'm going to say it again.

I'll love you forever and always.

I pinky promise...

Content Warning

Oh, hey there! I see you're wondering what exactly this book has in it. Here is the potential triggering subjects that are found in this book in no particular order. I'm fairly confident that I noted them all here, however, I'm human just like you and unfortunately that means I'm not perfect. With that being said I hope you enjoy the book!!!

Sexual Assault/Rape
Domestic Violence
Tones of Depression
Mention of drug use and overdose
Mention of death by cancer
Undertones of suicidal idealization
BDSM
Murder
PTSD
Anxiety
Reference to Christianity
Psychological and physical torture.
Homosexual and heterosexual intercourse

About the Author

M.R. Erfman is a certifiable ancient dragon slayer and a watermelon eating champion. Legend has it that she once arm wrestled a T-Rex for a London Fog and won. She may or may not own a time machine (long story, don't ask) and is frequently mistaken as an employee when visiting a bookstore. When she isn't traveling through the land of make believe she can be found talking to trees, contemplating how to write a serious bio, rolling critical failures with polyhedral dice, riding her motorcycle, and teaching her pets how to host a proper tea party.

www.ingramcontent.com/pod-product-compliance
Lightning Source LLC
Chambersburg PA
CBHW070458300726
48975CB00007B/2222